The characters and events portrayed in this book are fictitious. Any similarity to real persons, living or dead, is coincidental and not intended by the author. Any reference to real locations is only for atmospheric effect, and in no way truly represents those locations.

Copyright © 2023 by Ryan Casey

Cover design by Miblart

All rights reserved.

No part of this book may be reproduced in any form or by any electronic or mechanical means, including information storage and retrieval systems, without written permission from the author, except for the use of brief quotations in a book review.

Published by Higher Bank Books

PATIENT ZERO

A Post Apocalyptic Zombie Thriller

THE INFECTED CHRONICLES
BOOK 1

RYAN CASEY

GET A POST APOCALYPTIC NOVEL FOR FREE

To instantly receive an exclusive post apocalyptic novel totally free, sign up for Ryan Casey's author newsletter at: ryancaseybooks.com/fanclub

HAILEE

Hailee Westward knew something was wrong the moment she saw the man standing outside the entrance to the mortuary.

The corridor was dark. The light kept on flickering. Katya kept telling her she was going to find "a gap in the budget" to pay for a new lightbulb, which always pissed Hailee off. How much was a new lightbulb supposed to cost? How stretched *was* the NHS that they needed to reserve some of their budget to pay for a damned lightbulb?

The man stood outside the mortuary entrance. He was still. Swaying from side to side a little. It was dark down here—always dark down here. Because mortuaries didn't need natural light, did they? No, of course not. Whoever built this hospital hadn't taken the workers into consideration really, had they? Like, sure, dead bodies needed their rest. What was the point of light? And not like it wasn't already the most depressing damned job in existence. Spending her days with the dead. And then getting home, having some shitty overpriced microwave meal, falling asleep with a half-drunken glass of wine by her side, and then waking up feeling like death and doing it all over again.

And then there were the implications it had on the rest of her life. Dating. Yeah. Dating wasn't easy. Tell a bloke you work for the NHS, and they look at you with this patronising "oh gosh aren't you so nice and generous and caring" look that really means "when are we going back to my place to shag."

Tell them you work with the dead and their gaze shifts. Only an instantaneous thing, usually. Like, a microsecond of a thing. But it was there. In their eyes, you were a creep. There was something wrong with you. You were a bloody weirdo.

But still. Men being men, they still wanted to shag you.

But Hailee knew there were some men who wouldn't be able to get past the aura of death that surrounded her. And somehow... that gave her a weird sense of power that she didn't even understand herself.

And then there was her own family. The way Grandma always asked about Phil's job as a solicitor, always seemed so happy for him, so buzzing for him. But when it came to Hailee... she tried not to ask. Tried to gloss over it. Tried to change the subject if it came up because it creeped her out. Or just asked "all still okay with you?"

Sometimes, Hailee would say something inappropriate. She'd bring up the state of a body that had been scraped off the side of a road after a collision. She mentioned the way the man's head had caved in. The way it was all cracked, like an Easter egg that'd rolled down the hills on Easter Sunday when Granddad took her egg rolling. How bright red brain oozed out of the side of it, in horrible lumps of meat. And Grandma always went pale. She always got up and dashed—well, waddled—out of the room. And even though Mum and Phil always lambasted her for it... she got a kick out of it.

Of course, why show Hailee any sympathy at all? She'd chosen this career after all. She was reluctant when the post came up. She'd done a nursing degree. But she couldn't hack nursing. It wasn't the patients that were the issue. It was the women she worked with. Bitches. She never liked them. Gossipy. Clicky. Just not her people. Not at all.

So when the post came up, she jumped at the opportunity, as much as anyone *can* jump at an opportunity to work with the dead. Took a course to get her APT certificate, which took two years. Worked on some personal mindfulness regimens, so she wouldn't be quite as spooked by the dead. And, as they say, the rest was history.

The main appeal of the job? The dead couldn't bother you. The dead didn't bitch. The dead were... more manageable than the living.

But as she stood in the dark corridor, staring down at that man standing outside the mortuary door, for a moment, Hailee wasn't quite so sure.

He wasn't moving. He was just... standing there. Swaying from side to side. The light above him flickered, illuminating the dark corridor in a periodic glow. His breathing was heavy, raspy. Sounded like the death rattle. She thought of Granddad. Thought of his last moments, by his bedside. Thought of him holding her hand, digging his long fingernails into the back of her hand as he tried to cling on for dear life. That look of fear in his eyes. A look she'd never forget.

The look of a man who'd seen death. And didn't like what he was looking at.

She stood there in the corridor, and she looked at this man, and she wondered for a second whether this was what Granddad felt like, as he stared at death.

The man standing opposite her was called Jimmy Dalbrych. He was a construction worker. Lovely man, by all accounts. Never missed a day of work sick in his life. Family man. Two kids, who were his absolute world. Not the healthiest guy, sure. Always thought it would be the cigarettes that killed him, according to his wife.

Only it wasn't the cigarettes that killed him. It was another man. Someone on the site. Dimitri. One of the immigrants who didn't mix much with the others, apparently. Came into work one day and launched himself at Jimmy. Sank his teeth into his throat. Jimmy didn't stand much of a chance after that. As for Dimitri... nobody knew where the hell he was. Did a runner after the attack. Police trying their best to locate him. Might've done by now.

But still, it posed a question. One *serious* damned question.

Jimmy Dalbrych was dead. Hailee had just confirmed that—not that it needed much in the way of official confirmation.

So what was he doing standing outside the mortuary right now?

He stared at her. Kept on swaying from side to side. She couldn't see his face properly. The flickering, failing light made focusing difficult. And that was her first suspicion. It wasn't Jimmy. She'd had a long day, and she was tired. Working too much. That's what her friends always said to her. Ginny always told her she worked too hard, and spending so much time with the dead wasn't good for her—wouldn't be good for anyone.

And maybe that's what this was. This wasn't Jimmy. It was someone *like* Jimmy. Or someone playing a prank. The kinds of pranks she heard went down in medical school. Dentists being provided bodies to practice on. Dressing them up, taking them out to the dining hall, freaking the other students out. Sick. But kind of amusing, she had to admit. Hell, her sense of humour really had got dark since taking this job three years ago.

But... no. The whole someone playing a prank thing. That didn't add up. It didn't make sense.

Because Jimmy was standing there.

He was actually standing right there.

There was nobody behind him. Nobody next to him. He was on his own.

And he was looking right at her.

Breathing.

Another thought entered her mind. What if she'd messed up? What if the entire hospital had messed up? What if Jimmy wasn't dead at all? Stranger things had happened, right? You hear about bodies launching out of coffins on funeral days sometimes. Rare, but possible. But that always happened in foreign countries. Countries with poorer medical standards.

But right here? Right here in Britain?

This shit just didn't happen.

So why was it happening?

Another thought. What if she was imagining things? Maybe she really was losing the plot. Maybe the job really was getting too much for her. Maybe she really did need to settle down, find something different, something less stressful, something more conventional. Maybe she should give her mother those grandchildren she wanted—even though the thought of settling down with *anyone* made her avoidant hackles stand right on end.

She closed her burning-hot eyes. Heart pounding. When she opened her eyes, she wasn't going to see anyone standing there. When she opened her eyes, she was going to realise that she needed to see a doctor. That she had been hallucinating. And that she needed to see a doctor, and she needed to get on medication, and she needed...

When she opened her eyes, she didn't see Jimmy Dalbrych standing there.

She saw Jimmy Dalbrych *walking* towards her.

He walked with a shuffle. Like a baby deer—whatever they were called—walking for the very first time. His movements looked... They made him look like he was a puppet on strings. He jolted his neck to one side. Lifted a foot. Planted it down on the solid floor, leaving a blood print in his wake. He was naked. His skin was so grey it looked translucent.

But it was his eyes that really stood out.

She could see them now, as he got closer. Those brown eyes of his. There was something about eyes that really stood out to

Hailee. The difference between the eyes of the living and the eyes of the dead. The eyes of the dead... it was like a light had gone out. Like there was no power behind them. And that emptiness was something nobody could fake.

But Jimmy Dalbrych's eyes... they didn't have that light.

Jimmy Dalbrych's eyes were dead.

He took another step towards Hailee. His neck was torn. She could see the veins and the ripped muscle in there. It was impossible. Jimmy Dalbrych was alive. He was alive, and he was walking towards her.

But he couldn't be alive.

He wasn't alive.

This had to be a nightmare.

But it was a nightmare she was trapped in. And like every nightmare, it was one she had to escape.

"Jimmy," she said. She took a step back. What was she hoping? That he'd just suddenly snap out of this because she'd spoken to him? That he'd remember he was supposed to be dead, and collapse in a heap?

Jimmy didn't respond to Hailee's voice. Of course he didn't.

He just kept walking towards her.

And as he walked towards her, his steps grew steadier. They grew steadier until before Hailee knew it, he wasn't just walking. He was jogging. He was jogging towards her. And she had to turn around and she had to get away and she had to act fast or—or—

She spun around and went to run when she felt herself slipping.

The next thing Hailee knew she was on the floor. There was pain in her mouth, where she'd slammed against it. A yellow CAUTION: WET SURFACE sign right beside her, almost mockingly.

And the patter of those bare feet slapping against the floor behind her.

Shit. She needed to get up. She needed to get up because he

was chasing her. And even though it didn't make sense, even though it made no sense in her mind why he was chasing her or why he was alive or why she was scared... it was some primal sense inside her that told her she needed to get up and she needed to get away. Because something wasn't right.

She pushed herself to her knees when she felt the hands on her back.

She screamed. She swung her arms around as he held tightly on to her. "Jimmy!"

But Jimmy wasn't letting go.

He was holding on.

She didn't even know what she was doing. Kicking. Punching. Crying out. Screaming. All of it blending together in a haze. She was going to wake up. She was going to wake up and she was going to see this was a dream. It was an awful, vivid dream, and...

And then she felt him loosen his grip and suddenly she was standing again.

She saw the door up ahead. The security door. Get to that door. Type the code in. And then get out of this corridor.

She had a moment. A window. And she had to make that count.

She ran. She ran as fast as she could. Which wasn't all that fast at the best of times. But even worse now her knee was so sore after the fall. Shit. It was agony. Putting weight on it sent a million knives shooting through her body. She had to get to that door. She had to get to that door and she had to get out of this corridor.

She ran further. She could hear footsteps. She could hear panting. And she could hear this growling, too. This animalistic growl she'd never heard another human being make before. And she knew why she was scared now. It didn't make sense—none of it made sense—but she was scared, because he was alive when he should be dead, and he was after her, and she had this feeling deep in her gut that he was going to kill her.

She saw the door up ahead. Saw that keypad. The code. 4921. Or... Or was it 4922? Shit. She didn't have time to make any mistakes. She didn't have time to *not* make any mistakes. She didn't have any time at all.

She just had to get to that door.

She just had to...

That's when she felt something.

Around her right ankle. Tightening. And then before she could do anything about it, she fell towards the floor again. Cracked her head. Colours filled her vision. Everything went bright. Ringing split through her skull.

And before she even had time to process the implications of her fall, Hailee felt something else.

A sharp pain across her right thigh. Sharp, splitting agony, getting worse and worse.

And she didn't know what it was. It felt sharp. And then it felt achy. And whatever it was, it felt painful as hell, and she couldn't stop shouting, and couldn't stop screaming, and she needed help, and...

She looked over her shoulder and she saw Jimmy. He was holding on to her ankle. But he had his face buried down against the back of her leg. And she didn't get it. Not at first. She didn't understand why blood was pouring out of her leg. Was he kissing her? Some kind of creep?

And then he lifted his head up and she saw that dead look in his eyes.

She saw the chunk of meat between his teeth. Pieces of raw meat, falling out of his mouth. Blood spilling down his chin.

And Hailee didn't understand. Not at first. She didn't understand at all.

That meat. What was that meat? What was...

And then it all came together.

The pain in her leg.

The blood around Jimmy's mouth.

And that meat.

There was a chunk of flesh missing from her leg. It was bleeding. Bleeding badly.

Jimmy had bitten her.

Just like Dimitri had bitten Jimmy.

She screamed without thinking. And as she screamed, she heard the door behind her opening, and someone shouting something, something like "Get him off her!"

But all Hailee could do was stare into Jimmy's dead eyes, as he climbed up her body.

All she could do was look into those eyes, as he opened his bloody mouth.

And all she could do was scream, as he reached down and sank his teeth into her throat.

DAVID

***

David Watson closed the front door and sighed.

Another night shift in the bag.

His eyes were heavy. He knew he should probably eat something, but he didn't feel much like eating. He just wanted to get the hell to bed. His ears were ringing. Every footstep felt like he was dragging a damned ball along on a chain. That's what they call it, right? A ball and chain? Hell knows. He was knackered. He wanted his bed. That's all that mattered.

He walked into his lounge and threw his keys down on the floor. An empty bottle of Kraken rum lay on its side. Shit. Had he emptied the whole thing last night? Or... well, yesterday morning it'd be. Weird when you were on night shifts. Your sense of time got completely distorted. He'd got in from work—he was doing a few shifts on the doors at a nightclub in town, but it was very much a temporary gig, as was everything nowadays—opened the fridge door—the fridge door which was barely even hanging on at this point. Found nothing in there except for some out-of-date milk and a couple of ancient cloves of garlic. And then... Well, he saw the Kraken on the dirty-plate-laden kitchen worktop and the rest was history, as they say. A damned miracle he'd woken up in time for work at all.

He lifted a hand, rubbed his fingers through his thinning hair. To an outsider, his house might look like shit. There was a lot of clutter all over the place—but he didn't see it as clutter. He knew where shit was. People had their own systems. Well, David had his, too—and his was dumping everything on the floor.

He thought about Rina. Her disapproving face flashed in front of him, and disappeared all too soon. Yeah. She was one hell of a clean freak. No damned way she'd let him get away with this.

A lump swelled up in his throat. He swallowed it down. Yeah. Don't think about Rina. Not now. Not today of all days.

He kicked off his boots and walked through the lounge to the kitchen. Why the hell was he even heading into the kitchen? He hadn't done a shop since yesterday. He wasn't going to miraculously find a pizza waiting in here for him. Not anymore, anyway.

Rina sparked to mind again. Her smile. Her green eyes. Her laughter, as they sat in front of whatever shitty reality television show she fancied watching, pizza box on their lap. Just enjoying the small things in life.

A gaping emptiness swelled in the middle of his chest. A crushing fist, squeezing ever tighter.

Face it, David. Just face it. That's the past.

He opened the fridge, mechanically more than anything. The out-of-date milk was... even more out of date. The garlic cloves looked like they'd sprouted a whole new stem. Place could do with a good clean. He'd get to it. One day, he'd get to it.

Just... not today.

He closed the fridge door. Glanced across the kitchen worktop. No bottles of alcohol left. Damn it. Not even a drink to help him sleep. Not even a bit of booze to help him doze off. He needed a drink to doze off. Not that he had insomnia or anything, but... well, drink just helped dull the memories. Dull the thoughts. Dull the pain.

He gulped. Walked out of the kitchen, back towards the living room, where the television flickered. He kept it on all the time. Volume down. Made it feel less... well, lonely. Like there was someone else here.

But those people on the screen, they never turned to him. They never looked him in the eye.

Shit. How had his life come to this?

The meaningless moving images flickered on the screen in front of him. Rolling news. Some shit in Ukraine. A dam, destroyed. And then some shit about violence in London, and riots spreading across cities out of nowhere, and...

The photograph.

He saw it on the mantelpiece between a cigarette-filled ash tray and a few old bottles of beer. Staring back at him. He'd turned that photo round. He was sure of it.

So what the hell was it doing staring back at him now, today of all days?

He rushed across the living room, almost tripping on his dehumidifier, which he hadn't used in yonks. Grabbed that photograph without looking at it. He couldn't look at it. Especially when he didn't have any booze in. He didn't want to look at it. He didn't want it to get him thinking. He didn't want to start remembering...

He saw Rina. Her wide smile. Those beautiful green eyes. He was by her side. A younger, healthier, fitter version of his forty-nine-year-old self.

And between them...

He stroked Keira's face. Wherever she was, whatever she was doing right now, he hoped she was okay.

"I wish things could be different," he said. "I wish..."

And then he put the photo back on the mantelpiece.

He walked over to the sofa.

He planted himself down, in the saggy seat that perfectly formed around him, and he stared at the meaningless images on the television before him.

It took him a good few minutes of staring into empty space to realise what the headline on the television read.

ATTACK AT NORTH WEST HOSPITAL.

KEIRA

* * *

It'd been a relatively quiet night working on A&E—before the whispers about the hospital attack started.

Keira stood at the nurse's station. The vitals and patient information on the screen blurred together in a haze. She must be tired. Her vision always went all blurry like this when she was tired. Her eyes got really dry and itchy, too. Then again, of course she was tired. It was hardly surprising. She'd been working on A&E since nine last night. She was only supposed to be on til two. Sally, who was supposed to be in earlier, was sick. Nasty fever apparently, and uncontrollable vomiting. There was a vicious bug ripping through their staff lately. Keira just hoped she didn't catch it, too. She couldn't afford to.

The sterile air of the hospital emergency room felt... heavy. That was the only way to describe it. Heavy. You could almost taste the exhaustion of the rest of the staff. Keira always thought of it as a kind of hive mind, collectively weighed down by all the stress. She was so ready for home. Ready to tuck herself away in bed and... well, forget this place, for a few blissful, unconscious hours.

She glanced at her watch. Five to six. A tingle in her belly. A smile crept up the corners of her mouth. Almost time to go home. Almost time to make herself a nice, warm hot chocolate, then get in bed and sleep the day away.

And it was a good job. The info on this screen wasn't making any sense to her right now.

She rubbed her heavy, stinging eyes. Took a deep breath. Sighed. She looked over at the ward. At the old woman, Moira, sleeping soundly. At the young man next to her, whose name she didn't know. The rumble of chatter in A&E echoed through onto this ward, a reminder of the chaos she faced, every day and night of her life. It was peaceful on the wards. But A&E... A&E followed her everywhere. When she went home after work, she saw blood. She saw broken legs. She saw babies, choking.

A&E followed her everywhere. That was just a part of life she had to accept.

But she was getting to a point where she struggled accepting it.

No. No point thinking about that crap right now. Spent enough time lying awake thinking about it, exhausted in her bed. No need to start ruminating about it at work, either.

She looked around at the wall-mounted television in the ward opposite.

Some attacks in London. A riot, or something. Images of burning buildings flashed across the screen. Crowds of people flying into police officers, who desperately tried to hold them back. Across the bottom of the screen, RIOTS HIT BRISTOL.

Keira shook her head. What the hell was the world coming to? Seriously, shit had really hit the fan over the last few years. The coronavirus pandemic, which was an absolute hammer blow to the NHS—a hammer blow that the people in charge still weren't providing them with the resources to recover from. The war in

Ukraine, and the global tensions that caused. Honestly, Keira kind of wanted to switch off from the news completely. She had enough of a rough time at work without needing the extra worry about the state of the damned world on top of that.

And she had enough worry in the rest of her life to think about...

No. Don't think about that, either. Don't go there. Just don't go there.

She went to turn back to the screen to get the last of her work done when she noticed something on the television.

It was a new headline. Breaking News. ATTACK AT NORTH WEST HOSPITAL.

And seeing those words stretch across the bottom of the screen... Keira almost felt like she was imagining things. She was dreaming. Or she was reading it wrong. Her eyes, they were getting tired. She needed sleep. Hell, when was the last time she slept?

She needed to get home. She needed to get to bed. She needed to...

The door slammed open on her left. She jumped. Jean burst through, covered in sweat. Hell, Keira could smell her coming from a mile away.

"Have you heard?" Jean asked.

"I..."

"Down in the mortuary," Jean said. "There's been an attack. Some guy goes crazy. Goes crazy on poor Hailee down there. You know her?"

Keira shook her head. "I don't think—"

"They say it's like a nightmare down there. So much blood. And the guy who did it. He's done one. He's disappeared. Vanished. Into thin air."

Damn it. She was supposed to be going home. She was supposed to be finishing her shift. She didn't feel so tired all of a sudden. An attacker on the loose in the hospital? And all these riots across the country? What the hell was going on?

"And it ain't just here," Jean said.

"Huh?"

Jean waddled over towards Keira. She held her phone out in front of her. Her hands were shaking. "Blackburn. Blackpool. Manchester. Liverpool. Birmingham. Riots. But attacks, too. Hospital attacks. So many hospital attacks."

Keira watched Jean scroll down that greasy screen with her chubby fingers. Hospital attack after hospital attack. A tightness squeezed across her chest. What was happening? What was going on?

A bang to her left. The rattle of a trolley against the tiled floors. Shouting. Screaming. Panic.

"Nurse! Doctor! We need—we need a doctor!"

A cleaner raced towards her. He looked pale. His eyes were wide. He ran across the corridor, pushing someone along in a trolley.

Keira looked down at the person in the trolley, and she expected to see a woman sitting there. This "Hailee" woman, who had been attacked.

But it wasn't Hailee.

"Omar," she said.

Omar—a cleaner she got on great with—was lying on the trolley.

Blood spurted from his neck, trickling down the side of the trolley, and onto the floor.

He gasped and gargled.

His eyes pulsated, threatening to burst out of his eye sockets.

"Please!" the hospital worker shouted. "He needs help!"

Keira stood there at the nurse's station. She watched the panic unfold in front of her. She saw the television screen above. *ATTACKS SPREAD NATIONALLY.*

A nudge against her left wrist. Her watch alarm, notifying her that her shift was over.

She took a deep breath of the clammy air, and she sighed.

Somehow, Keira didn't think she was heading home from work just yet.

NISHA

* * *

Nisha watched Mrs Thompson waving her hands through the air at the front of the classroom and she wanted to go home.

She was tired. Kept yawning, which she knew was naughty even though she didn't know why. Mrs Thompson never liked it when people yawned, even though Nisha didn't understand because she wasn't yawning because she was being rude; she was just yawning because she was tired.

She looked up at the clock above Mrs Thompson. The little hand was pointing to the 9, and the big hand to the floor. Which meant it was early. The little hand needed to move all the way round to the 3 for it to be home time.

And today wasn't just a normal home time. Today was the home time before non-uniform day tomorrow, and toy day, and then it was the summer holidays.

Nisha smiled when she thought of the summer holidays. She was going to go to Blackpool with Dad next week. They were going to ride rollercoasters together. She was big enough to go on the Big One now. She smiled at the thought of it. Some other kids said rollercoasters were scary. That they didn't like how fast they went. They screamed when they went down the drop, because they didn't like the way it made their belly feel.

But Nisha didn't know what screaming was. Because she couldn't hear.

She watched Mrs Thompson waving her hands across the class as she went on about Maths. Nisha didn't like Maths. She found Maths boring. But Dad always told her to listen during Maths, because if she didn't listen in Maths she'd end up cleaning like him.

Nisha didn't know why Dad told her cleaning was bad. Nisha liked cleaning. And it was important for things to be clean. If people didn't clean, then the world would be so dirty, and nobody liked a dirty world.

So Nisha thought of Dad like a superhero. A superhero who cleaned up the world.

She loved Dad. She loved him a lot.

She saw Mrs Thompson gesturing at her.

Nisha. Am I boring you?

Nisha opened her mouth. Went to respond. A little sound must've come out, 'cause she could see the other kids looking at her, laughing. Mrs Thompson's eyes were really wide. She looked angry. But she looked tired, too. Her eyes were red, like Dad's were when he came in from working late nights cleaning at the hospital. Her face looked white, too; white like a ghost. And she was shaky. Her hands weren't moving as fast as they usually did. Something was wrong.

Nisha?

Sorry, Nisha signed.

You will be sorry when you get extra homework for the summer holidays.

Mrs Thompson's mouth moved when she signed these words. Which meant the other kids knew what she'd said, too. They all started laughing. She couldn't hear them. But she could see them smiling. She could see Connor Best wincing, like he knew how painful these words would be to Nisha. She could see Lucinda De'Bright giggling and saying something to Helen, who Nisha hated. Nisha's face grew hot. She wanted to disappear into a hole in the ground.

Dad wanted her to go to a special school for deaf children. But he didn't have the money. People didn't get a lot of money for cleaning up, apparently. Other kids teased her for what her dad did, too. But their dads did boring stuff, like things with numbers, and in boring offices. Her dad did something good. Her dad was the best.

Mrs Thompson kept on waving her hands and Nisha tried her hardest not to yawn again. But trying hard not to yawn made her want to yawn even more. She wasn't going to be able to hold this yawn in all day. She was going to have to make it to break and then let out the biggest yawn in the world.

Suddenly, the head teacher, Mr Rawford, walked in. He was a little man who always looked sweaty and smelled like baked beans. He walked over to Mrs Thompson and he whispered something to her. Mrs Thompson's eyes widened. She nodded at him. She looked around at the kids. Her eyes were wide and even more red. She touched her hair and she folded her arms. And Mr Rawford, he kept on wiping his shiny, sweaty head.

Something was wrong.

Mrs Thompson looked around at the class. She said something to them, but she didn't sign. And then she rushed out of the classroom.

The other kids looked at each other. Their mouths moved. Connor Best smiled, and banged against the table. Lucinda and Helen covered their mouths. And Nisha wanted to ask what was going on. Mrs Thompson never ran out the classroom like that. And the kids, the rest of the kids, they looked worried, excited.

She got up. She walked across the class. She needed to ask

Mrs Thompson what was happening. Mrs Thompson didn't look well. She must've forgotten to tell Nisha what was going on because she was sick.

She walked over to the classroom door. She poked her head around the corner. Mrs Thompson ran along the corridor. One hand on her belly, the other over her mouth. And then she disappeared into the girl's toilets.

That was weird. Because Mrs Thompson didn't usually go in the girl's toilets. She usually went in the staff toilets, where only teachers could go. First, Mr Rawford, the head teacher, looking all worried. And now... Mrs Thompson.

What was happening?

She looked down the corridor between the classrooms. She couldn't see anyone else about. A few shadows from the Year 4 class. The door to Year 5 shut, when it was normally open. The drawings on the wall. Drawings that her and the other kids had done. The sandpit, and the computer area, where they went to play boring games sometimes.

Nisha turned around. She looked down the corridor, towards the toilets. She was supposed to ask before she went to the toilet. You weren't allowed to just walk out of the classroom and to the toilets without a teacher's permission.

She took a deep breath, which made the butterflies in her tummy flutter away a little.

And then she walked down the corridor, towards the toilets.

She tried to walk quietly, even though she didn't know what quiet was. Dad said she had "elephant feet" when she was running downstairs. He always heard her when she sneaked to the kitchen for snacks in the night, even though she tiptoed her way down. So she went even slower than that now. She didn't want anyone to hear her. She didn't want to get in trouble.

She reached the bathroom. Stood there. Looked at the door to the girls' toilets. Her heart was beating fast, like when she was on rollercoasters last time, the last time when Dad got kicked off because he hadn't paid, because he couldn't afford it. Only this heartbeat wasn't good. It was bad. It was scary.

She took another deep breath. Smelled the school dinners in the air. Mash potato. Veg. Meat. The other kids took lunchboxes in. Dad couldn't afford it, so said she had to take the free school meals. They weren't that bad. The other kids teased her for it, but the joke was on them because she loved turkey twizzlers.

Dad always said she was brave. So brave. Braver than she even realised. She didn't believe him. She didn't feel brave. She felt scared. She'd never admit that to the other kids or to anyone, but she always felt scared. And she always felt weak, too. Because she couldn't hear. She couldn't hear, and that made her weaker. That made her… much weaker than everyone else.

But right now, she took another deep breath.

Right now, she was going to go into the toilets and she was going to check on Mrs Thompson.

Right now, she was going to be brave.

She walked over to the toilet door. Reached up. Put her hand against the greasy wood. She looked around. Back down the corridor. Nobody around. It was so quiet. She might not be able to hear, but it just *felt* quiet. Something felt wrong.

She turned back to the door. Pushed it. Felt it shaking—creaking, probably.

And then she stepped inside.

The bright light above her flickered. A load of dead flies sat inside it. The floor was all wet. And the smell of cleaning stuff which reminded her of Dad filled her nostrils. The walls looked like they were white once, but they were a dirty brownish colour now. The sinks were covered with old bits of soap, and wet bits of blue paper towels.

And over on the right, Nisha saw one of the doors was open.

She saw a glimpse of darkness within. A shadow, moving in there. As she walked towards it, a metallic scent wafted through the air, making her nose crinkle.

She walked over to that door. Stopped, right before it. The light flickering even more than normal now.

Just walk towards it. Just walk around that corner. It'll be okay. Everything'll be okay.

She took another breath of that metal-smelling air.

And then even though the deep breaths didn't make the butterflies disappear anymore, she stepped around the front of that door, and she looked inside.

When she saw what was in front of her, Nisha realised two things.

Firstly, that something was definitely wrong.

And secondly, she was right to feel afraid.

Very afraid.

DWAYNE

* * *

Dwayne ran as fast as he could and didn't look back.

His heart raced. His stomach tingled. He felt excited. But at the same time, he felt... afraid. Consequences. The consequences of his actions. They were going to catch up with him. At some point, they were going to catch up with him.

But for now... that didn't matter.

The only thing that mattered?

Getting away.

He glanced at his cracked watch. Ten a.m., sharp. He pulled the rucksack over his shoulder. Where the hell was his ride out of this place? Nico was supposed to meet him here, right by the library. Ten a.m., not a moment earlier, not a moment later.

But there was no one here.

He felt hot. The fabric of the balaclava rubbed against his face. He couldn't wait to drag it off. Couldn't wait to feel the air against his skin.

But not now.

He could feel that symphony of unrest swirling around him on the streets of Preston city centre. The air crackled with tension, the vibrations of anger and frustration palpable in every shout and every shattered window. Something was happening in the city. Riots, erupting like wildfire up and down the country. He didn't know what people were rioting about. He didn't really follow the news. But he'd heard the police talking about it on the radio he'd hacked. Talking about how all their units were stretched already. Talking about an incident at the hospital—a critical incident—and how all backup units were needed down there immediately.

Only there were no backup units. The backup units were already preoccupied.

Perfect day for a robbery.

He looked down the road. Flames flickered in the distance. The smell of smoke and burning filled his lungs. Shouting bounced around his skull. He didn't know what was happening. And really, he didn't care. It'd caused a distraction. A perfect distraction. An opportunity to do what he needed to do. To carry out the robbery he'd been planning for the best part of a year.

It was simple on paper. Walk into a bank with a pistol. Force the staff onto their knees. Break into the cash machine—already pre-hacked—grab the money, then run. But there were so many more intricacies than that. Making sure the CCTV was out on your escape routes. Having a disguise—a different change of clothes—for both legs of the journey; for the entrance and the exit. A bank robbery wasn't a thuggish endeavour. A bank robbery was an exercise in patience, a masterclass in planning, and a symphony in execution. Especially these days, when it was harder to commit and get away with a crime than ever.

And Dwayne had delivered that masterclass perfectly.

But his getaway vehicle wasn't here. Nico was supposed to be here. The Serbian bastard was always late. He knew he'd end up late. Nico even joked about it himself sometimes. Serbs. Never on time. It wasn't racist because Dwayne didn't think it. It was Nico who'd thought it.

And he was leaning right into that stereotype right now.

He looked at his watch again. Still ten. Unsurprisingly. Shit. Where the hell was Nico? He might be a lazy bastard. But he stood to gain as much from this robbery as Dwayne did. They'd planned it. Right down to the minute. So where was he?

He looked over towards the main hustle and bustle of town. He heard more shouting. Sirens echoed against the buildings. His cheeks heated up. Maybe they were coming for him. Maybe they were already onto him.

A man and a woman ran past. Both of them kept looking over their shoulders. The man was limping. His leg was bleeding. The woman, who had short curly hair, held on to him. "Just keep running, Danny. We'll get you to the hospital. It'll be alright."

And somehow, Dwayne didn't think either of them would be getting to the hospital. The man, 'cause he was bleeding like mad. And the woman, because she looked... sick. Really sick.

He'd heard the rumours about the mystery illness over the last few days. New strain of COVID, some were saying. Others, a bad bout of the flu. Coughing. Sickness. Dizziness. Some of them throwing up blood.

And these riots. A part of him wondered whether they might be something to do with this virus. Maybe people were getting anxious about the prospect of another lockdown. Those lockdowns worked during COVID, sure. But things had changed. Compliance wasn't going to be anywhere near as good if they locked down again. Especially after the government messed up so badly last time round, breaking their own rules. If they asked people to stay at home and save lives again, the people were gonna give them the middle finger.

And there were other issues, too. A cost-of-living crisis the likes of which no one had ever seen. The price of bills soaring through the roof. Parents struggling to put food on the table for their kids.

Dwayne pulled the rucksack further over his shoulder. He wasn't gonna have many money issues anymore.

A man screamed up the street. Dwayne looked around. Some old dude, limping along. Some young hoodie jumped on his back. Wrestled him to the ground. "Please! Please! Argh!" Shit. That old dude needed help.

But...

Screw him. Nobody had given him any favours in recent years. It was old bastards like him who forced him into the position he was in. Having to steal. Having to rob banks to survive. Okay. Maybe an exaggeration. But he had his reasons. And they were reasons he'd rather not think about.

He turned away from the screaming old bastard and he looked up the street when he saw something that made him smile.

A black Range Rover hurtled towards him.

"Nico," he said. "You late bastard."

The Range Rover slowed down, its engine growling as it got closer. And Dwayne felt this sudden twinge in his chest. This tightness in his fists. This clamminess in his cheeks. Something didn't seem right.

The old man screamed out. Dwayne glanced around at him and...

Shit.

He was bleeding. And he was bleeding badly. Very frigging badly. The hoodie sitting on top of him... Wait, was he fucking *eating* him? What the hell was going on? What the hell was—

"Hey."

A voice.

Dwayne spun around.

And then he saw Nico sitting there in the driver's seat. Staring out the window at him. He was a handsome bastard, a source of much of Dwayne's envy. The girls all loved him.

But right now he looked pale.

He looked sick.

"We need to go," Nico said, his forehead dripping beads of sweat. "We need to get out of here. Now."

Dwayne looked back at the two men on the ground. The hoodie, staring over at him, with this dead-eyed gaze. Blood oozing down his chin. The old man lying on the road, twitching. Swinging his flailing old arms up at the hoodie, the life draining from his body.

And then he heard sirens, and in the distance, he saw police cars.

"Now!" Nico said.

Dwayne swallowed a lump in his throat. He pulled the rucksack further over his shoulder.

And then he rushed around to the passenger side of Nico's car, and he climbed inside.

When he looked out through the back windscreen, he saw that hoodie standing there. Blood dripping down his face. Chewing.

Watching him.

PETE

* * *

"It's bad, Pete. Like, really frigging bad. People ripping each other's faces off bad. You've no idea."

Pete put his foot on the accelerator and tried to drown out Stan's droning on. Preston was going to shit today. The whole frigging country was going to shit today. Started with riots. Riots in the cities. Violent attacks, many unprovoked. Unrest in the cities. Violence in the hospitals. Nurses attacking patients, and patients attacking nurses. Something was wrong. Didn't take a genius to figure that much out. But it was damned confusing. And it was damned overwhelming. And Stan's droning on wasn't helping. Not right now.

"Marco," Stan said, his voice quivery, shaky. "He messaged me. Look."

"I can't look," Pete said. "I'm driving."

"You're driving. My bad. Sorry. You're driving. He... I'll read it for you. What he saw. Let me just... let me just find it... No, that's not it. That's not it. I'm on to Moira now. Oh shit I've called her. I've..."

He droned on some more, and Pete did his best to focus on the road instead. The city of Preston loomed small in the distance. His own little personal joke, that. "Loomed large." That's what people usually said, wasn't it? Well, it was impossible for a city like Preston to loom large. There were no skyscrapers. Hell, there weren't even any tall buildings. The most impressive building in Preston was the bus station. Brutalist masterpiece, apparently. Pete didn't know what that meant. But it looked like shit to him. The amount of junkies he'd locked up there, the amount of kids he'd taken down to the station... hell, he'd lost count. But it was enough to put him off that place for a lifetime.

It was early for a riot. Pete hadn't been in many—fortunately. But riots he'd seen on telly and in the news always seemed to kick off at night. For one to be going down right now, ten in the morning, in a city that it was an understatement to call "sleepy"... yeah, something was definitely off.

He gripped the steering wheel tight and pushed harder on the accelerator. The radio kept on buzzing—reports of incidents all over the damned place. He'd switched off from that, too. Because he had somewhere he needed to be.

The police station.

To lock up one of his nemeses.

He glanced in the rear-view mirror and saw Colin Helm sitting on the back seat. That junkie little prick had been an absolute pain in Pete's arse for the last two years. Petty crime. Drugs offences. Domestics. Theft. In and out of prison. Waste of space. Absolute waste of air. What was the point sending a shit like that to prison again? He'd only get out and get himself back into trouble again.

Today was different.

Because Colin Helm had killed someone.

His girlfriend.

Colin's eyes were bloodshot. Tears streamed down his sore-covered face. His teeth chattered. He kept mumbling shit under his breath. "I had to," he said. "She—she came at me. I had to."

Pete gritted his teeth and smiled. He was going to take this wanker back to the station. He was going to lock him in the holding cells. And he was going to be the one who was there with him for the interview, to present the evidence to him, when the day arrived.

He glanced up in the rear-view again. Saw those wide, haunted eyes. That pale, sweaty face.

"I had to. She—she wouldn't stop. She wouldn't stop."

"Shit!" Stan shouted.

Pete glanced at the road. Saw someone standing there, right in the middle. He swerved the car, narrowly dodging them.

"What the hell are they doing standing there?" he shouted, slamming on his horn.

Pete gasped. "We should go back," he said. "Arrest them while we're at it."

Pete looked up in his rear-view. Saw that figure standing there, right in the middle of the road. "What the hell's got into people today?"

"Mandy thinks it's that flu going 'round. Thinks it's messing with people's heads."

"That's funny," Pete said. "Helen thinks it's Russia. Chemical weapon, or something."

"Helen?" Stan said.

Pete's cheeks heated up. "Yeah. Helen."

Stan froze. Like he was about to ask Pete another question, a question too far.

"Wives and their conspiracy theories, right?"

Phew. "Right. They have no idea people are just batshit crazy."

Stan chuckled. Pete didn't like taking the piss out of Helen. 'Cause clearly something was wrong. People didn't just riot for no reason, out of the blue. And the attacks at the hospitals... he'd heard some grim shit. What the hell was going on with that?

"Once we've dropped junkie features back there off at the station," Stan said, "where we heading?"

A knot tightened in Pete's chest. "We should stay with him for a while. Monitor him."

"Monitor him? We're needed everywhere, Pete."

"Maybe so," Pete said. "Let's just get this done before we start thinking about anything else, right?"

He saw how Stan looked at him. Those narrowed eyes. Bastard. Judgemental bastard. Pete had tried calling Helen an hour back but he couldn't get hold of her. And that wasn't like Helen. She was usually glued to her phone. And with all the riots and all the looting going on... he was even more worried.

He looked back in his rear-view at Colin. He looked paler than ever. Shivering violently. And he smelled. Smelled bad. Like shit.

"Damn," Stan said. "Has junkie features back there dropped one?"

"He'll be dropping plenty more when he finds out how long he's going down for."

"I—I had to," Colin gasped. "I had to."

Stan waved him off. "Yeah, yeah. You keep on going on about how you 'had to' do it, lunatic. See what a jury says about that."

Pete saw cars up ahead. Traffic. He flicked on the siren, but none of the cars were moving. There was nowhere for them to move. He couldn't drive around them. And then people were getting out of their cars. Running down the side of them. Looking over their shoulders. Tripping up. Running away from something. Fear in their eyes.

"You keep banging on about how you had to do it," Stan said, his voice drifting back into focus. "And you'll pay for shitting yourself in our car, too. Understand? You'll pay for it."

Stan looked back in the mirror at Colin. Shit. He really didn't look well. His skin was translucent. He shook even more violently than before. And that smell. That smell of shit. It had another smell to it, too. Almost like an earthy smell. The smell of the ground after a storm.

"Please," Colin said. Gripping his own thighs so tight his dirty long fingernails looked like they were on the verge of piercing his skin. "You don't understand—"

"I think I do understand," Stan said, leaning back, stuffing his face right into the back of the car. "You're a junkie. And now you're a murderer. And you're getting cold damned feet about what you've done. 'Cause you're realising what kind of a shitty life's waiting ahead for you inside."

Pete saw more people running past. He heard more screaming. He heard glass smashing. He heard footsteps banging against concrete. He could feel the temperature outside rising. He sat there in his uniform and he knew he needed to get out. He knew he needed to help.

But, Helen.

He pulled his phone out. Tried tapping her name again. Phone rang, and rang, and then cut out. Where was she? And what was happening here?

He hit his siren again. Tried to drive around the mass of cars and people now. People chasing people. Rioters chasing people. He needed to get out. He needed to help. He needed to—

"I had to!" Colin shouted. His voice echoed around the interior of the police car. "I had to because—because she bit me. She bit me and she wouldn't stop biting. And—and I tried to push her away. I tried to get her off me. But then she bit me again. On my stomach. On my chest. And she kept biting and biting and I had to... I had to..."

Pete saw it, then.

He saw the blood seeping through Colin's dirty blue T-shirt.

He smelled it, metallic in the air. Coppery.

And then he looked up into Colin's eyes, in that rear-view mirror.

"She bit you?" Stan said. "What the hell are you..."

And then, out of nowhere, Colin opened his mouth, and he projectile vomited a stream of deep red blood all over Stan's face.

DAVID

* * *

David stared at the television screen and read those words again and again.

ATTACK AT NORTH WEST HOSPITAL.

The local hospital. That was where Keira worked. Or at least it was where she worked the last time he'd spoken to her anyway. Which admittedly was a while ago. Years ago, in fact. She was a nurse there. A&E nurse the last time he'd checked. She loved her job. He was so damned proud of her. She always wanted to be a nurse. Always wanted to care for people. Always wanted to make a difference.

His chest swelled with warmth as he thought of his daughter, and where she might be now.

And then a punch split through his gut, as he read those words again.

ATTACK AT NORTH WEST HOSPITAL.

The news anchor's mouth moved, but David couldn't hear any words. Her eyes were wide. She kept glancing down at the desk in front of her, then over her shoulder, breaking the illusion of authority inside the newsroom. Something was happening. Something big. The riots. The hospital attacks. And now here. Right here in Preston. Shit.

He reached into his pocket, fumbling around for his phone. Shit. Where was it? He needed to call Keira. He needed to call her and he needed to know she was okay. But if he couldn't find his bloody phone, he couldn't bloody call her.

He looked around the living room. The blue-ish glow from the television filled the curtained darkness. Where'd he put it? Shit, had he left it at work? If he had, he was screwed. Working security at a nightclub was *not* the place for leaving your phone lying around. Ash, one of the other bouncers, was a phone thief. No chance David was ever seeing that phone again if he'd got his greasy fat mitts on it.

He looked everywhere for it when he remembered. The drinks holder of his car. He'd put it in there. He'd forgotten to bring it in. That's all it was.

He raced over to the front door. Turned the handle. Yanked it open. Stepped outside, into the bright sunlight. Ran into the driveway. Peered in through the car window, and…

There. There it was. Sitting right there in the drinks holder.

He clicked the unlock button on his car key. Pulled the handle.

The door didn't budge.

"Shit," David said. "Not now. Not frigging now."

He clicked the unlock button again. Tried the door again.

Nothing.

"Fucking hell." Not now. His key had been playing up for a good few weeks now. Or the locking system. Hard to tell. Kept meaning to take it down to the garage to get looked at. But taking it to the garage for it to be looked at meant interacting with people. And he hated people.

He clicked it again and again, kept on trying the door, his phone tantalisingly close, when suddenly he heard an engine.

An engine, revving up. Hurtling down the road.

Boy racer, probably. He lived on a country lane just off the main road, so he did get them down here.

But the car that went past. A Honda Jazz. And then another car. Fiat Punto. They didn't look like boy racer cars. And the people in them. He didn't get a proper good look at them, but they didn't look like boy racers, either. One couple looked old.

Weird. Probably unrelated to the hospital attacks; to these riots breaking out across the country. One was kicking off in town just before he headed home. Yeah, he wasn't sticking around in town for that.

But there was something bothering him. He couldn't put his finger on it. But he just had this feeling. This sense.

A sense that it was related.

A sense that something was very wrong.

He clicked the unlock button again and his car made a beep.

"Finally."

He pulled open the door. Grabbed his phone. Tapped the screen.

Black.

Dead. Shit. Shit, shit, shit. Out of battery. Why today of all days was he out of battery?

But then of *course* he was out of battery. He was always out of frigging battery. His phone was shit. He needed a new one—apparently. That's what Ash always told him at work, anyway. Of course he did. Probably sell him a stolen one.

He slammed his car door shut. Paced up the driveway, back towards the house.

A scream echoed down the road.

David stopped. Froze. Looked over his shoulder. That scream. It sounded like someone was in trouble. Big trouble. He lived on a quiet road. Never any trouble down here.

So why was someone screaming?

He shook his head. "Not now. Not now."

And then he walked back inside his house—and he locked the door, for good measure.

He ran into the living room. Now he just had to hope his charger was where he thought he'd left it.

"Please be here," he said, searching the sofa. "Please be here, please be here, please be…"

It wasn't there.

"Shit."

He ran through into the kitchen. Pulled open every drawer. Where was the frigging thing? Where the hell was it?

He pulled open the last drawer.

A little notepad stared up at him.

An idea sparked in his mind. He had a landline phone he never used. And… this notepad. There was something in this notepad that could help him.

He turned the pages, right to the middle.

And then, there in the middle, he saw it etched in black pen.

KEIRA: 077928273427

Phew. He had it. Only… was that last number a seven or a one? Shit. He'd try both if he had to.

He ran into the living room. Grabbed the landline. *Please work. Please fucking work…*

A dialling tone.

"Thank God for that."

He keyed in the number with his shaking fingers. Outside, he heard another scream. Somewhere in the distance, an almighty crash erupted through the silence.

But David just focused on the number.

"Four… two… seven."

A pause.

"Come on. Come on…"

"I'm sorry, but the number you are calling is not recognised."

"Shit. It's a one. A frigging one."

He cancelled the call. And then he dialled the number again.

Hit a two midway through. Deleted it, forgot where he was up to, had to go back to the start again.

He took a deep breath. Closed his eyes. Pull yourself together, man.

And then he opened his eyes. Dialled the number.

"Four... two... one."

Another pause.

A pause longer than the last pause.

"Come on, come on, come—"

"I'm sorry, but the number you are calling is not recognised."

"Shit!" David shouted.

He slammed the phone down. No luck with either number. A lump swelled in his throat as he pictured Keira's face. She must've changed her number. Changed her number, and severed the final thread of communication between them.

He wished things were different. He wished he'd done things so much differently.

Maybe this is your chance.

He looked up. Up from the landline. Up towards the curtain-covered windows. Yes. That was it. He had to go to the hospital. He had to go out there and he had to find her. He didn't have her number. He couldn't just sit here and twiddle his thumbs. Even if she didn't work at the hospital anymore... he couldn't just give up. He had to try.

She was his daughter. And no matter what'd happened between them, he still loved her.

He stood up. Ran upstairs. Grabbed a rucksack from underneath his dirty clothes, which were spread across the floor. He pushed his duvet aside, saw his phone charger. Typical. Just bloody typical. He threw a few things into his rucksack. Change of clothes. First aid kit. That sort of shit. And as he stood there in the middle of his bedroom, with no real idea of what he was doing, of what he had to take, there was only one thing he knew right now. One thing, clearer in his mind than anything else.

He had to get to the hospital.

He had to find his daughter.

He ran towards the bedroom door when suddenly he saw something.

Outside his dusty, bird-shit-laden bedroom window. Didn't see it at first. Just caught his eye as he was walking away.

But when it caught his eye... his stomach sank.

He walked towards the window.

Looked out onto the overgrown, weed haven of a garden.

Mrs Kirkham, his next-door neighbour, stood motionless.

She was naked.

And she was bathed in a macabre crimson.

Blood.

KEIRA

* * *

Keira knew her night shift was well and truly over.

But there was absolutely no way she was walking away from the scene in front of her.

Omar, the cleaner, clutched on to his bleeding neck. Blood gushed out of it, dripping down the side of the trolley and on to the tiled floor below. Omar writhed in pain. He was usually so full of life. Usually so friendly, and happy-go-lucky. A nice man. A family man. Thought the world of his daughter, whose name evaded Keira right now.

But there was no trace of that man in front of Keira.

His eyes bulged, threatening to burst out of his skull. He gurgled blood, and gasped, like he was drowning. He gripped hold of Keira's arm, digging his long nails into her skin.

"It's okay, Omar," Keira said. "It's okay. You're going to be okay. I promise you're going to be okay."

"Can we get a doctor here?" Jean shouted. But no one responded. A scream echoed through the ward from A&E. An old woman stood at the entrance to this private room they'd taken Omar. "What's happening?" she asked.

"I wish I could tell you," Keira said. "I wish I could tell you."

Omar's eyes bulged wide. Keira pressed her blood-soaked hands against his neck to try and stop the flow while they waited for someone more qualified to come to their aid. But was anyone coming to their aid? Was anyone going to help Omar? Shouts and screams echoed through the corridors, mingling with the emergency room's chaotic cacophony. Keira's heart pounded in her chest. The whooshing sound of her heartbeat burst through her skull. She was supposed to keep calm in moments like this. She was supposed to keep her cool. That was her job.

"I'm gonna have to go get someone," Jean said.

"What?"

Jean looked down at Omar. Her eyes glistened with tears. "Omar. I'll find someone, Omar. Someone who can come help you."

"But you can't leave me to—"

Jean grabbed Keira's shoulders. Leaned right up to her. "You're strong, sis. You're strong, and you're brave. And right now Omar needs you. Okay? Omar needs you. And I need to go find help. I need to find help, and I need to put the patients at ease. Okay? 'Cause—cause something's happening here. Something bad. And we're nurses. We're nurses. And we're here to help."

No. Jean couldn't go. Keira couldn't be alone. Because—because—

"Don't think about Blackpool," Jean said. "Don't even think about it. Okay? 'Cause that wasn't your fault, sis. That wasn't your fault. So don't even go there."

The screams.

The blood.

The dizziness, and the panic, and...

No. Don't think about that. Don't think about Blackpool. Not right now.

"You've got this. Okay? You've got this. You do what you've got to do. You be a nurse."

As much as Keira didn't want to... she nodded.

Jean nodded back at her. Then she ran over to the door.

"Jean?" Keira said.

Jean turned around. "Huh?"

"Come back," Keira said. "Please, please come back."

Jean's eyes widened. She nodded. And Keira didn't really understand why she'd said what she'd said. She didn't fully understand what she meant herself by "come back".

But it was just this sense inside her. This feeling.

A sense that Jean was in danger.

They were all in danger.

And then Jean opened the door and ran out into the chaos.

Keira turned around. The side room she was in wasn't silent. But she felt... she felt alone. She felt so alone.

Omar writhed around on the blood-soaked trolley. A stream of blood oozed out of his neck, between his long, shaking fingers. He glared up at Keira, moving his lips, trying to say something, choking on his own blood.

Keira put a hand to his head. His skin was on fire. Shit. A fever. She'd seen a few fevers like this the last couple of days. In the young and fit as well as the old. There was a nasty bug going round. Could this be the bug? The source of all the pandemonium here at the hospital tonight? Tensions spilling over? Resources so stretched that things were getting out of control? Were the people finally rising up against the government? Was enough finally enough?

She looked at the bloody wound on Omar's neck. Severed veins spurted blood like water pistols. She pressed her hand against his neck. Applied pressure to stave the flow.

"Come on, Jean. Come on. Please. We need a doctor. Please."

And then, out of nowhere, Omar lifted his right hand. He placed it on the back of Keira's neck. Keira jumped a little. Those fingers were so cold. Icy cold. His face burned like fire, but his fingers were like ice blocks.

Omar looked into her eyes. Tears rolled down his cheeks, mingling with the blood.

He opened his mouth. Strained it open. His tongue twitched. His yellow teeth chattered.

"Nisha," he gasped. "My... my Nisha. Make sure... make sure..."

And then his eyes rolled back into his skull.

"No," Keira said. "Omar. Omar. No. Don't..." She turned around. "Help! Someone help!"

She turned back to Omar. Pressed down on his neck. "Omar. Please hold on. For Nisha. Hold on. For her. For... Omar!"

But Omar wasn't breathing.

Shit. Shit, shit, shit.

This was Blackpool again.

The blood.

Feeling frozen to the spot—unable to move, unable to—

No.

She needed to check his vitals. She needed to keep him alive. She couldn't let him die.

She wiped tears from her eyes. Put her shaking fingers to the back of his wrist. She couldn't feel a pulse. But she couldn't feel *anything*. She had to get him hooked up. Get his vitals checked. She had to...

She looked down at Omar. The whites of his eyes glared up into nothingness. Blood trickled out of his open mouth. His writhing had stopped, and he was still. Very still.

And Keira knew. She knew what this meant. She didn't have to hook him up to any machine to discover the inevitable.

He was gone.

Omar was dead.

Keira buried her head in her blood-soaked hands. She cried. The ground opened up beneath her. Darkness surrounded her.

Shouts filled the hospital. Bedside alarms rang everywhere. And she was alone. She was completely alone.

"I'm sorry, Omar," she gasped. "I'm sorry I failed you. I'm sorry I fail everyone. I'm sorry I…"

And then, Keira heard something that made the hairs on the back of her neck stand on end.

Right in front of her, where Omar was lying, she heard shuffling.

And then she heard something else.

Something even more paralysing.

A deep, guttural growl.

NISHA

* * *

Nisha stared into the bathroom cubicle and she felt sick. The light above flickered. Flies buzzed around. A metal smell filled her nostrils and made her dizzy. Her hands shook. Pretty purple colours appeared in front of her eyes, like when she was at the cinema and she couldn't breathe properly that time and Dad held her hand and told her to breathe, just breathe.

But right now she couldn't just breathe.

Mrs Thompson crouched down on her knees. Her bum pointed up in the air. She looked sick in class. Pale. And sweaty. And she'd run out of class and right to the girls' toilets, so she must be ill.

But this...

She was being sick. The smell of the sick was different to the smell of sick Nisha remembered. She was ill over Christmas. Dad cooked turkey, and Gran brought some of her nice biscuits, but they weren't nice biscuits, they were horrible and dry and they made Nisha sick everywhere in the night.

The smell was so bad. Like that cheese Mum used to buy when she was around. Mum bought that cheese on the last night Nisha saw her. She remembered opening her eyes. Smelling the cheese and knowing Mum was home from work at the job she didn't understand. Only she saw Mum creeping away with some man. Taking Dad's wallet, then disappearing. And Nisha didn't understand. Just that Dad kept shouting the next day, smashing plates, then crying. And she was so hungry. But she wanted to look after him. She wanted to make sure he was okay. Because she loved him. And he loved her too.

Mrs Thompson crouched on her knees. Nisha needed to get out of here. She needed to go. She wasn't well. And Mrs Thompson wasn't going to be happy if she knew Nisha was out of class without permission.

Nisha took a step back when suddenly, Mrs Thompson lifted her head.

She turned around. Fast. Looked right into Nisha's eyes.

Blood oozed down Mrs Thompson's chin. There was all red blood on the sides of the dirty toilet, too, dripping down into the water. That reminded her of Mum, too. Going into the bathroom and finding all blood in the toilet. Mum telling her it was something that would happen to her too, when she was older. That women were cursed. Nisha didn't understand her at the time. She still didn't.

But looking at Mrs Thompson now, maybe this was what Mum meant about women being cursed.

Her eyes were all red. It looked like little red bombs had exploded in there, and made them bleed inside. There was even blood coming out of her ears. That couldn't be good.

Mrs Thompson's lips moved. She was saying something to her. Trying to speak to her. But Mrs Thompson knew Nisha couldn't hear her. She was one of the best teachers at sign language. What was she saying? What was she trying to tell her?

And then Mrs Thompson lifted her hands. Bloody handprints

dripped down the toilet seat. She raised her hands, slowly. Her bony fingers shook like they were freezing cold.

What did she want to say?

What did she want to tell Nisha?

She moved her hands. But it was all blurry to Nisha. It was all so blurry, as she waved them in front of her. *Read? Right? Rich?* What was she trying to say?

I can't understand, Nisha signed. *I can't...*

And then she saw what Mrs Thompson was saying.

She saw what she was signing.

She saw exactly what she was trying to tell her.

She felt her body freeze. Like ice was covering her. She'd got it wrong. She'd understood wrong. She couldn't be signing *that*. But Mrs Thompson's lips... she could see them moving and that's what it looked like. That word was exactly what it looked like.

What? Nisha signed.

Mrs Thompson spun around. Her head twitched. More blood splattered down the sides of the toilet this time, missing the bowl. On the floor, a thick blob of meat sat amidst the puddle of blood. Nisha tasted burning in her throat. Just like when she was sick at Christmas. Dad. She thought of Dad, sitting by her side, stroking her hair. *It's alright. You're going to be alright, my baby.*

Mrs Thompson lifted her head.

She wasn't moving anymore. She was still. Very still. She wasn't shaking anymore, either. Maybe she was better now. Maybe she just felt sick and she needed to throw up. Maybe everything was okay now.

And then she turned around.

Slowly.

Nisha's heart raced. Her knees wobbled. She needed a wee. Really badly. She didn't think she'd be able to hold it in.

Mrs Thompson's head turned even further. Blood on her chin. Little blobs of thick meaty blood dropped down onto the floor. But she wasn't shaking anymore. And...

Her eyes.

She looked at Nisha. Something was different. Something was wrong. The way she looked at her. It was like...

Like Nisha wasn't there.

Mrs Thompson lifted her hands.

She waved them through the air.

And she signed that same word she'd signed just before.

A word that sent a shiver up Nisha's spine.

Run.

And then Mrs Thompson jumped to her feet, and she launched herself at Nisha.

DWAYNE

* * *

"You look like shit," Dwayne said.

"Yeah, I mean, I'm picking you up from an armed robbery. I forgot to do my hair."

"Valid."

"Thanks for the approval."

Nico really did look like shit, though. His skin glowed white, like Casper the Ghost on a bad day. His teeth chattered. And was that saliva trickling down his chin?

"Have you taken something?" Dwayne asked.

"'Taken something'? Seriously? You've just robbed an ATM in a bank and *that's* what you're bothered about?"

"I care about your health, Nico. Is that really such a crime?"

"Piss off. Did you get it all?"

Dwayne felt the weight of the rucksack pressing down against his legs. "I got as much as I could."

Nico slapped Dwayne's back, swerving the car a little. "Good man. That's my boy."

"Will it be enough?"

"If you got what we agreed, it'll be enough," Nico said.

"And once this is done... we're out? Completely?"

Nico wiped his running nose with the crusty off-white sleeve of his shirt. Hell, he really did look like shit. "If that's what you want, my boy. But why stop at this? There's a whole world of opportunity out there. Streets are going to shit. Maybe we could start today."

Dwayne looked out the passenger window. Smoke rose from the distant buildings. A smoggy cloud hovered over town, a blot on the clear blue skies. He stared into the distance, beyond the confines of the city. Today was the day. The day he paid off his debts and got out of this business, once and for all. And it wasn't a false alarm this time. Pay off his debts, take his cut, and then get on the first flight out of this country to the Costa Del Sol. Spend a life in the sun. A new life, away from all the demons of his past.

"I mean, look at all these cars," Nico said. "I bet a few of 'um have a hundred or two in the glove compartment."

Dwayne looked around. Traffic built up ahead. But a lot of the cars looked... empty. Like the drivers had got up and abandoned them.

"This to do with the riots?" Dwayne asked.

"Riots. Some sickness. Attacks at hospitals. Hell, who knows? I just know one place you *don't* wanna go is Ribblesdale Court."

"I knew that *before* it started kicking off."

"Seriously," Nico said. "Look at what this wanker did to me back there."

He lifted the leg of his right short.

"Holy shit," Dwayne said.

Blood oozed out of Nico's leg. Nico laughed. "Gross, huh?"

"Are those—"

"Toothmarks? Yeah."

"Some arsehole bit you on the leg?"

"That's why I was late."

"Did you piss him off?"

"Did I piss him off? What kind of a question is that?"

"You usually piss people off."

"Okay. Maybe I usually piss people off. But... no. No, I didn't piss him off. Not that I know, anyway."

"So a man just comes up to you and bites you on the leg?"

"Just like that," Nico said.

"So what did you do?"

"What did I do? I kicked the bastard off me and I got into the car and I drove."

"And you don't think that bloke might call the police or something?"

"What, you wanted me to stay with him? Report him? Besides. Nah. He was off his face on spice or something. Never seen anyone that *gone*."

Dwayne felt a knot in his stomach. Something was really off. The riots. The hospital attacks. "People are going crazy."

"Tell me about it," Nico said. "It's just a good job that guy had the shittiest, most ground-down teeth I've ever seen in my goddamned life, or I'd be in..." He sneezed. A massive sneeze, deafening Dwayne.

"Shit," Dwayne said. "You mind covering your face when you do that?"

"What? And let my hands off the wheel?"

"You need two hands to cover your face?"

"Yeah. Cause I produce a shitload of snot. See."

Nico leaned over and rubbed a load of snot in Dwayne's face.

Dwayne punched his hands away. "Gross. You dirty bastard."

Nico laughed. But then his laugh turned into a cough.

"Seriously, though," Dwayne said. "If you don't mind me saying—"

"You usually say that when you're about to say something I mind you saying."

"You don't look well. Maybe you should get it checked at the hospital or something."

Nico laughed. "Scuse me, doctor. Just on a getaway drive for my bank-robbing friend. Some weirdo bit me, and I've got a cold. How's that gonna go down?"

"If you ask it like a dumbass like that, then probably not well."

Nico shrugged. A little blood seeped through his shorts. "Seriously. Chill, pal. You've done the hard part. Now you've just gotta trust me, haven't you?"

"That's the hard part."

Nico turned and glared at him. "Rude."

"You know what's even ruder?"

"What?"

Dwayne nodded ahead.

"Shit," Nico said. "Junction's blocked."

He wasn't kidding. A wall of cars blocked their route out of here.

"We're just gonna have to wait—"

"We can't wait," Nico said, pulling his phone out of his pocket. "Call Mobeen. My phone's messing up."

"Call *Mobeen?*"

"Call Mobeen. Tell him we've got his cash and we're stuck in traffic."

"Genius idea," Dwayne said. "How about we give him another reason to take an even bigger cut of the cash while we're at it?"

"That might not be such a bad idea. Deal sweetener, or whatever."

"No chance," Dwayne said. "I'm not giving up any more of *my* money."

"Then what do you suggest, genius? I barge my way through here?"

Dwayne looked over his shoulder. There were cars behind them now, too. "Shit."

"What?"

"We're blocked in."

"Blocked in?" Nico said. "We'll see about…"

Suddenly, Nico stopped speaking. He stared out the window. His eyes widened.

"Nico?"

Nico wasn't moving a muscle. His eyes bulged out of his skull. What the hell was going on?

"Nico," Dwayne said. Behind, a driver slammed on his car horn. Crap. Not now. He needed Nico fit and well. He needed to get the hell out of here. The longer he sat here with this money on his lap, the more risk he was in. Because there were rival groups out there, too. People who wanted this money just as much as he did.

But something was happening to Nico.

Burst blood vessels wormed through the yellowing whites of his eyeballs, filling them deep red. His grip on the steering wheel loosened, and his hands fell to his side.

And that's when the blood started oozing out of his ears and his nostrils.

"Nico!" Dwayne said. Shit. What the hell was happening? The bite. The bleeding. And now this.

Shit.

Shit, shit, shit.

Dwayne grabbed Nico's shoulders. But Nico just slumped to the window, cracking his head on the glass.

"Nico? What... what..."

And that's when Dwayne heard it.

A tap on the window.

He turned around, half-expecting to see an angry driver trying to get past.

"Yeah, yeah," he muttered. "I'm kind of a bit busy h..."

It wasn't any angry driver.

It wasn't a police officer.

It was something far, far worse.

PETE

* * *

Pete leaned back in his seat and tried to wrap his head around what in the name of God he was looking at.

Colin opened his mouth and projectile vomited all over Stan's face. But it wasn't just normal vomit. No sir. It was blood. Dark crimson. All over Stan.

Stan sat there in the passenger seat of the police car. Blood dripped down his face. The buzz of the radio was the only thing that broke through the silence. Stan looked shocked. His eyes were wide. His lips kept moving, but no sounds emerged. And Pete mighta found it funny. In some circumstances, he mighta found it quite funny. Stan was as serious as they got. One of those fellas who could dish it out no end, but the second anyone took the piss out of him, it was game over. He'd been the same ever since Pete first joined the force. "*Don't piss him off,*" Carla told him at the time. "*Trust me. You don't want to get on his bad side.*"

And Pete found that out first-hand soon enough. Stole Stan's locker keys. How rough could he be? It was only a practical joke. And he worked in an environment where practical jokes were an everyday occurrence. Couldn't take yourself too seriously in the police, or the weight of some of the shit you had to deal with would just get way too much.

But he'd never forget the moment Stan walked in. Exploded with anger. Started throwing papers everywhere; slinging keyboards across the office. Funny at first. But the longer it went on, the more Pete realised he was gonna have to own up to being the culprit.

And the way Stan looked at him when he told him. When he held out those keys to him. He felt like he was the suspect in a murder investigation. Not someone who'd just played a damned practical joke.

Stan had that look on his face right now.

He pressed his shaking fingers to his face. Pulled them away, looked down at them, wide-eyed. When he saw the blood, his eyes widened. He glanced up, over his fingers, over at Colin.

Colin didn't look well. His eyes rolled back into his skull. Bloodshot eye whites bulged out of his head, twitching. He looked like he was having a damned seizure. Blood oozed out of his mouth, down his chin, dripping onto the squad car's plush leather seat. It wasn't just his eyes, either. Blood trickled out of his ears. And his lips looked bitten.

Like he was gnawing at them.

"Colin," Pete said. A knot tightened in his chest. What the hell was going on? Bad batch of drugs. Had to be a bad batch of drugs.

But... No.

Something was different.

Something was *wrong*.

"Colin," Pete said. He needed to get back there. Colin... He didn't like the prick. Couldn't wait to get him locked away in a cell —for good this time.

But at the same time, Colin was in a bad way. The bleeding.

The eyes. Pete didn't know what the hell was going on, but he knew he needed to help the guy in some way.

Before he could act, Stan lunged into the back of the car.

He grabbed Colin around the throat. Pulled back his fist. "You think that's funny do you?"

"Stan," Pete said.

Stan swung a fist into the side of Colin's head—hard. "You think it's funny do you, huh? You murderous prick. You murderous bastard. Yeah. Let's see how funny you find it now. Let's just see."

Stan swung at Colin again. Repeatedly. Shit. Stan could be rough with the shitheads sometimes. He'd had a few slaps on the wrist for conduct in his long stint in the force.

But this...

This was brutality.

He was punching a defenceless bloke. A defenceless bloke who was having some kind of seizure.

Pete needed to do something.

"Stan," he said. He grabbed his arm. Yanked it back.

But Stan just swatted him away, like he was an annoying fly. He glared at Pete. His bright white eyes burned through that red face. His nostrils twitched. *Shut the fuck up. Back the fuck off.* That's what that look screamed at Pete.

And then Stan turned around. Started beating Colin again.

Pete's heart raced. God damn it. How could he stop this? Stan was stronger than him. Once he was in the zone, there was no stopping him.

He heard a scream outside and saw a brunette woman running past. Blood spilled out of a nasty wound on her arm. She looked over her shoulder, eyes wide with terror.

Horns honked all around. Cars tried to navigate their way around each other. A long-haired man on a motorbike drove up between two lorries, only for one of those lorry drivers to open their door, send the rider tumbling to his arse.

And seeing it all. Seeing it all unfolding before him. Pete felt a sense of duty. He felt this instinctive desire to maintain order. To protect people. Because he was a police officer. And that was his job.

But there was this other feeling, too.

Helen.

He'd tried calling her, so many times. Tried, and failed to get through.

The riots. The attacks. The sudden disorder.

And now...

His radio buzzed to life.

"We've got an attack at the station!" a fuzzy voice shouted. "It's Genevieve. She's ripping Andy's face off. With her teeth. Something's happening. She started vomiting blood and then—and then—she's—she's—"

Static swallowed the voice. The sound of Stan's fists cracking against Colin's face came into focus.

And as Pete sat there, as he listened to the static of the radio, as he listened to the screaming outside, and as he pictured Genevieve ripping Andy's face away...

She started vomiting blood...

Pete swung around. "Stan..."

Stan's fist froze mid-air, as he clutched on to Colin's throat.

He scowled at Pete.

"What?" he said. "What the hell do you..."

It all happened so fast.

Colin threw himself at Stan.

He grabbed the sides of his head.

And then he sunk his teeth into the side of his face.

DAVID

* * *

David saw Mrs Kirkham standing there in the middle of his garden, covered in blood.

She stared up at him. Into the window. Her long, grey hair dangled down the sides of her shoulders, splattered with blood. Her eyes twitched relentlessly. Wait. He could only see the whites of her eyes. Couldn't see her pupils. Must've rolled around in her head.

She was a pretty good neighbour, by all accounts. She was getting on a bit. Lost her husband, Bill, a few years ago. Ever since then, she clearly struggled with the loneliness. Whenever David was in the garden doing pretty much anything, she'd soon be out there, bobbing her head over the fence, asking what he was up to, asking him around for a brew. He'd always tell her he was too busy. That he had too much on. Kind of felt guilty for it in truth. She was just a lonely old woman who needed some company. Maybe he could've been better with her.

And now, she'd had some kind of accident. She'd had some kind of accident, and she was standing in the middle of his garden. Was it bad that his first instinct was that he was gonna end up bogged down chatting to her for God knows how long? He was never gonna get her off his property.

But... No. The blood on her face. Her eyes, twitching white in her skull. Mrs Kirkham wasn't in a good way. She needed help.

That burning urgency filled David's body. Keira. His daughter who may or may not work at the hospital was potentially in danger. He had to get to the hospital. He had to try to find her.

But Mrs Kirkham...

She needed help. Something had happened to her. Something related to the attacks spreading across the nation like wildfire? No. No, there'd be no riots or kicking off down this road. It was quiet. Rural. People didn't kick off down here.

But if that's not what it was... what was it?

And then Mrs Kirkham started to walk towards his house.

She shuffled down the garden. Her legs buckled under her minuscule weight. Her body shook with every step. She stared ahead. Towards the back of David's house.

Shit. She was going to knock on his door any moment now. It was usually the fence she rattled on, whenever she needed to alert him about... well, about *anything*. A dead bird at the bottom of her garden that turned out to be very much alive. A rat on her decking, which was nothing more than a pile of leaves.

But now, she was in his garden, and she was walking towards the back door.

"Shit," David muttered. He turned around and he walked out of the bedroom, towards the stairs. His trip to the hospital would have to wait a few more minutes. Which was shitty. He didn't want to waste any more time. Every second he wasted was another second Keira could find herself in more danger.

But what was he supposed to do? Ignore the blood-splattered old lady walking across his garden? He knew what Rina would say, if she were here. She'd tell him to "love thy neighbour". And what would David say in return? *"You're supposed to be Hindu, not Christ-*

ian." Stupid, but one of those running jokes they always had whenever neighbours and friends were concerned.

He reached the bottom of the stairs. Saw Rina's painting sitting on the wall beside the front door. The abstract piece. David used to always tease her for it. Tell her it looked like random different things. *Nice muffin,* he'd say. *Squirrel's looking particularly gorgeous today.*

And it used to piss her off no end. *It's art. You should learn to look past your crappy TV shows and appreciate it.*

At least I know what's happening on my crappy TV shows, he'd say. Always won him a thump on the arm. And ironic, considering she loved reality TV. A woman of many contrasts.

Then that numbing emptiness, exploding in the middle of his chest. The same sensation that always accompanied the memories of the past. Bittersweet.

"I miss you," he whispered.

He turned around. Walked down the hallway. Pushed the kitchen door open. He hadn't heard any knocks at the door yet. Was she still shuffling her way down the garden?

He stepped into the kitchen.

Pots towered everywhere. Flies buzzed around the remnants of some old bean juice, encrusted to one of the plates. A faint hint of sour milk wafted through the air.

And outside the back window, Mrs Kirkham was nowhere to be seen.

David saw the tall grass. He saw the mass of weeds. But Mrs Kirkham... there was no sign of her. Just her bloody footprints, right there in the grass.

Where was she? Where had she gone?

"Mrs Kirkham?"

He crept through the kitchen, towards the window. She was out there just moments ago. And she definitely didn't look like she was moving all that fast.

So where was she now?

He leaned up to the window. She wasn't out there. Grass. Weeds. Dying plants, dying since the day Rina... since the day Rina went away. But no Mrs Kirkham.

Wait. How'd she got in the garden in the first place? She was an old woman. She needed a stairlift to get up to bed at night. So how'd she got into his garden?

Blood trickled down one of the fence panels on the left, bordering her house.

"What the hell is this?"

That's when he heard it.

Shuffling.

To his right.

He turned around. Looked over through the little doorway that led to the back door, and the utility room.

"Mrs Kirkham?"

Silence.

A shiver rushed down David's spine. He'd heard something. He'd heard movement. So why wasn't she responding? What the hell was happening?

He crept towards that doorway. His feet creaked against the loose wooden floorboards. "Mrs Kirkham?"

More silence.

He reached the doorway. Stopped. Froze. He strained. Strained to hear her. To hear *anything*.

But he couldn't hear anything at all.

His heart pounded in his chest. His face felt hot, clammy. Was he afraid? He felt afraid. But why was he afraid? She was just an old woman. An old woman in need. That's all there was to it.

Right?

He swallowed a lump in his throat.

Stepped through the doorway.

That's when he saw it.

First, the back door. Open. He hadn't left the back door open. He was pretty sure of it.

So Mrs Kirkham must've opened it.

And then he saw the bloody footprints.

Bloody footprints, stepping through that doorway.

Into the utility room.

And then...

Wait.

Those footprints.

There were more footprints.

Fainter footprints.

And they led right into the kitchen.

Right past...

And that's when David heard the noise that sent another shudder right down his spine.

Right behind him, in the silence of the kitchen, David heard a growl.

KEIRA

* * *

Omar stared at Keira, and she just... she just didn't understand.

He was standing. He was standing and he was alive. But she'd checked his vitals. She'd checked his vitals and she hadn't felt a heartbeat. She'd checked his vitals and he was gone. Dead.

Unless she was mistaken. She was panicking after all. Maybe she'd got it wrong. Maybe there was still a pulse. Maybe in the panic, she was mistaken.

But even if she was mistaken—which she must've been—one thing was for sure.

Omar shouldn't be on his feet right now.

Blood gushed out of the gaping wound on his neck. He wasn't applying pressure to it anymore. He wasn't gargling, or choking, or trying to fight it. And his eyes... there was no fear in his eyes anymore.

His eyes looked... dead.

She remembered Blackpool. The panic. The fear.

And... those eyes...

No. Not Blackpool. Not right now.

Blood waterfalled from Omar's gaping throat. He stood there in front of Keira, swaying from side to side. His lips twitched. A rattling groan sneaked out of his throat. It was like he was trying to say something. And when he groaned, Keira saw his vocal cords twitching in his open neck.

Alarms rang out through the hospital. Distant screams echoed through the wards, down the corridors. The panic and the tension surrounding her was palpable.

But her focus was Omar.

"Omar?" she said. Her voice cracked.

Omar didn't move. He just stood there. Staring blankly at Keira.

"You need to get back on the bed, Omar," Keira said. "You've had a nasty injury. You need to get back on your bed right now."

But Omar didn't budge. He just stood there. Swaying. Blood oozing down his neck, down his chest, dripping down onto the red-stained floor.

That wound. That gaping, open wound on his neck. People didn't survive wounds like that. Especially not without proper medical attention. And they definitely didn't shoot up to their feet moments after looking like they'd died from blood loss.

She remembered what Jean told her. The attack. And then the news of the attacks at hospitals across the country. The attack in the mortuary. The riots. Everything.

Was it all linked, somehow? And even if it was... why would anyone hurt Omar? He was a lovely man. Family man. Absolutely doted on his daughter, Nisha.

And there was something else, too. This knot in her stomach. The same feeling she had when she was in a nightmare, hard to explain, impossible to describe.

The same feeling she'd experienced in Blackpool on that fateful day.

Only...

No. This was different.

This was fear.

This was pure fear.

"Omar," she said, shaking. "I'm going to need you to lie down. I'm worried you might be—"

And then he flew at her.

He grabbed the sides of her face. Pushed her off her feet. Pain split through the back of her head as she landed on the solid floor with a crack. She could hear screaming somewhere, and she realised it was coming from herself.

Omar pressed her head against the floor. He squeezed his hands around her temples so tight she felt like her skull might just explode. Rusty, metallic-tasting blood gushed all over her face.

And those eyes.

Those bloodshot eyes...

They reminded her of Uncle Joseph.

They reminded her of—

He opened his mouth and moved his teeth in towards her neck and—

And she punched him. She was holding something. Holding something she'd grabbed from her side, she had no idea what, and she wasn't even thinking, she was just in the moment, just purely in the moment and—

Omar tumbled away.

She lay there. Frozen. She couldn't move. She couldn't breathe. She was going to throw up. She was going to...

Omar swung his neck around towards her, like a ragdoll dummy springing back to life. Those vacant, glazed eyes peered at her with growing anger. Blood pooled even more freely from his neck, down towards the stained hospital floor. Above, the lights flickered. Alarms rang out. Screams echoed.

No. She couldn't just lie here. She had to get up. She had to get out of here. Because as much as she had a duty of care to Omar... Omar wasn't himself. Omar just attacked her.

And if she hadn't cracked him over the head when she did...

Shit. She didn't want to *think* about what might've happened.

She stood up, lunged towards the door. Pulled the handle. She had to get out of here. She had to get out of here and—

Something gripped around her right ankle. Yanked her back.

Omar.

It was Omar.

She looked down at him. He held on to her ankle. Dug his long, sharp, dirty fingernails in so deep she could see blood. He opened his mouth again. Pulled himself towards Keira's ankle. Trying to bite her again. What was with the biting today?

She didn't want to hurt Omar. But instinct kicked in. He was trying to bite her. And even though it didn't make sense... *he'd* been bitten, and now look at him.

No. That was bullshit. It had to be bullshit. What was she thinking? He was a frigging *zombie* or something? Zombies only existed in fiction. Zombies only existed in shit TV shows with tired tropes. Zombies weren't a real thing. Zombies weren't possible.

But this maniac was trying to bite her.

And she didn't want to take her chances.

She lifted her foot and she booted him in the face.

Hard.

It went against all her instincts. Her duty of care. Her role as a nurse. Her general reluctance to violence. It flew right in the face of all of those, just like her foot flew right into Omar's face right now.

Omar tumbled back. His teeth snapped together. He didn't look up at Keira. He just hurtled towards her leg again, like he was an animal fixated on its prey. There was no emotion in what he was doing. There was just...

Hunger.

She kicked him again. His nose cracked.

"I'm sorry, Omar."

And then she opened the door and she ran.

She didn't look where she was going. She just legged it. Legged it down the ward. She heard crying. Screaming. She heard shouting. An alarm echoed through the corridors. On her left, a woman sat on top of an old man, Bill, whose bloods Keira had taken multiple times today. Her jaw was clamped around his throat. Blood splattered everywhere. Bill slapped his hands against her. Scratched at her back. Screamed. But the woman wasn't going anywhere.

Keira turned away. Run. Just run. She couldn't breathe. This was a nightmare. This was a fucking nightmare. This was a bad dream. This wasn't real. This couldn't be real. This had to be a bad dream.

A bang echoed right behind her. A shout, making the hairs on the back of her neck stand on end.

She turned around. Looked over her shoulder.

Omar flew out of the side ward. He was completely covered in blood now. And he was screaming.

Screaming.

And flying towards her.

"Fuck!" Keira said.

She turned. Ran. Tripped. Time stood still. She was going to fall over. She was going to hit the floor. She was going to hit the floor and she was going to die and—

She kept her balance.

Kept running.

A door. A door ahead of her. She didn't know where she was. Lost all sense of where she was. All sense of everything.

She just had to get through this door.

She just had to get away.

She yanked the handle open and she heard a new scream.

She didn't want to turn around. Didn't want to look. Didn't want to see.

But she turned anyway.

A nurse. One of the new ones. Gavin, he was called. Nice lad. Jean said he was a star.

He was on the floor.

Omar was on top of him.

And he was ripping the skin away from Gavin's stomach.

Gavin screamed.

Blood and intestines wormed through his torn scrubs.

He looked over at Keira, stretched out his quivering hand.

"Please!" he screamed. "Please!"

Keira wanted to help him. She had to help him. He was on the floor. He was bleeding out. He needed help.

But... the screaming.

The alarms, ringing.

The violence.

The savagery.

The blood.

Keira shook her head. Her vision clouded, and her eyes stung. "I'm sorry," she said. "I'm sorry."

And then she swung the door open, slammed it shut, and ran.

Keira was so distracted by the pandemonium that she didn't see the sign written above the door.

MORTUARY.

NISHA

* * *

Mrs Thompson jumped to her feet and launched herself out of the toilet cubicle at Nisha.

She reached out her hands. Opened her blood-splattered mouth. There was all blood in the cracks between her teeth, which looked yellower than Nisha thought they were. She was never an angry teacher. She never got mad at her class. Not like Mrs Wilkinson did. She used to get so mad all the time. And she was rubbish at sign language, and she always said it was just Nisha who was rubbish at understanding sign, and that maybe her dad wasn't teaching her properly, which made her confused and made Dad annoyed.

But she looked angry now.

Nisha tried to run out of the way when Mrs Thompson grabbed her. She pushed her back against the wall. She felt something smash behind her. Mirror. And her back. Her back cracked right against the sink. She'd pushed her so hard she felt sick.

She opened her mouth. Tried to speak. Tried to shout—but she didn't know whether she was speaking or shouting at all. Mrs Thompson, she pushed her back further and she opened her mouth and she leaned in towards her, like a dog, like an angry dog trying to bite her. Nisha used to like dogs. Until one bit her. A big yellow one. Snarled at her. Bit her. And she was scared of dogs after that. Had loads of nightmares about dogs biting her, eating her, gobbling her up whole.

She didn't know what to do. A warmth filled her pants, and she realised she was weeing. The smell of pee filled the air, like when she used to wet the bed sometimes just as an excuse to get in Dad's bed. She felt comfy in Dad's bed. She felt safe in Dad's bed. There were no monsters in Dad's room. None at all.

She lifted her hands as Mrs Thompson held her back. She waved, shaking, right in her face.

Please Mrs Thompson please don't hurt me I've not been bad please.

But Mrs Thompson pushed her back harder.

Pushed her further against the wall.

Nisha couldn't move. She couldn't speak. She was stuck, and Mrs Thompson was hurting her, and she didn't know why she was hurting her because Nisha was always good for her, she was always nice, she always did her work her best, and...

Mrs Thompson opened her mouth.

She moved her teeth towards the middle of Nisha's face, like a shark on one of those programs Dad watched, attacking the little fishes.

"Please," Nisha tried to gasp. "Please..."

She squeezed her eyes shut and thought of Dad.

Thought of his smile.

Thought of his cuddles.

Thought of his bedtime stories.

And then...

And then something happened.

Or rather, nothing happened.

Nisha opened her eyes.

Mrs Thompson looked right into her eyes. She looked like she was *smelling* her. Like she was a polar bear like on that YouTube vid Dad showed her, smelling its prey. Nisha loved animals. She loved the scary animals best.

But she didn't like Mrs Thompson right now.

She sniffed at Nisha. Blood drooled from her lips with spit. She smelled bad. Like metal and sick and something else that Nisha didn't think she'd ever smelled before. Like mud mixed with sweat mixed with...

And then Mrs Thompson let go of her.

Dropped her.

Nisha didn't look up. She didn't turn around to Mrs Thompson again. She just turned on the spot and ran.

She ran out the flickering light of the bathroom. She ran down the corridor. She had to get to class. She had to tell them Mrs Thompson wasn't well. She wasn't well at all. She was sick. She was very sick.

She looked down the corridor, towards the other classrooms. One of the doors that was shut before was open now. She couldn't see anyone in there. That was weird. They were meant to be in the middle of class. And the door was shut before. So why was it open now?

And where were they all?

She ran back into class and she wondered if they'd left her. If they'd all left her, and it was just her and Angry Mrs Thompson in here now.

She opened the door to her class and ran inside when she saw them all sitting there.

The class. Her class, all sitting there in their seats. All looking up at her. All frowning. Muttering to themselves.

Nisha tried to sign.

Mrs Thompson sick. We need to go. Danger.

But they all just looked at each other and laughed and started waving their hands in the air.

Nisha's face went hot. They were laughing at her. She was trying to help them and they were laughing at her.

She needed to try harder. She needed to do better. She needed to be braver. She needed...

She opened her mouth. Forced air out. Moved her lips how it looked like people spoke, squeezing her eyes shut when she did. Darkness. Just darkness, and her.

She thought the words. Thought them, in her head. Saw them, right in front of her.

Mrs Thompson sick. Attacked me. Need to go. Something wrong.

She saw the kids in her mind. Saw them all nodding. All running away with her. All thanking her for helping them. Dad being so happy with her when she got home. So proud. Getting a certificate in a big assembly for being so brave, and everyone clapping, and having so many friends, and...

She opened her eyes.

The kids were all laughing at her.

Nicola Hilton went cross-eyed, opened her mouth in funny shapes, stuck her tongue out.

Brad Harvey waved his hands in the air and drooled.

Nisha looked at them all laughing at her right now and her eyes went all clouded, like when she was watching that movie Coco, and it made her all sad. Her cheeks burned. And she had this other feeling, too. A feeling in her chest.

A vision.

A flash of them all being attacked by Mrs Thompson.

Of her tearing them all to little pieces.

She took a deep breath.

Turned around.

And that's when she saw it.

The whiteboard. The old whiteboard, which Mrs Thompson never used anymore.

She could write on there. She could write on there and she

could tell the other kids what was happening. She could help them.

She ran over to the whiteboard. Looked around for a pen. Couldn't see one. She looked around even more. And then she found one. Right by the side of the board.

She grabbed it. She pulled the lid off. She started to write, and...

The pen wasn't working. It was dry.

No!

She threw it down. She looked at Mrs Thompson's drawer. She knew she wasn't supposed to go in there. But she needed to check. She needed to check. She couldn't give up—even if it got her in trouble.

She pulled the drawer open and she saw it staring right up at her.

A pen. A whiteboard pen.

Yes. This had to work. It just had to work.

She grabbed it. She pulled the lid off. And she started writing on the board, not really thinking of what she was going to say...

Red ink.

Red ink, on the board.

Yes. It was working. It was working. She could help.

She tried to stop her hand shaking. She wrote the words, as fast as she could, as neat as she could—and she wasn't the neatest writer in the class, so it wasn't easy.

Mrs Thompson sick. Attacked me. Blood everywhere. Need to go. Now.

She stepped back. Looked at the warning she'd etched on the whiteboard.

And then she turned around to the class and raised a hand to point at it.

When she looked... she didn't understand. Not at first.

She blinked. Blinked again. She could feel her heart bumping fast. Even bumping in her head now, which was weird 'cause she didn't know you could feel your heart in your head.

But...

Even though she blinked, it didn't change anything.

The classroom was empty.

The kids had all gone.

She stood there. Shaking. They were there. They were there when she last looked. Where were they now? Where had they gone?

She went to turn around and run out of the classroom when she felt something that made her tummy turn inside out.

A hand.

Grabbing her arm.

Tight.

DWAYNE

* * *

"Well, buddy. Fancy seeing each other here on a day like today, hmm?"

The "something far far worse" that stood at the car window was a man called Gary. Dwayne had the misfortune of knowing him well. He used to run with him, Nico and a few others. Drugs, mostly. But a spot of human trafficking here and there, too. Light stuff. Nothing too serious.

But then Gary stabbed the lot of them in the back. Starting running with the Albanians. Even though the Albanians were definitely just using him, and he was just too dumb to see it.

But Gary being here right now was a problem. A problem he could do without, with Nico lying unconscious beside him, and stuck in this mass of traffic, and... and *something* going on out there. All while he tried to get away with his cash.

"Gary—"

"Don't 'Gary' me," Gary said.

"What do you want me to say? Harry?"

"Smart arse," Gary said, with a distinctly Eastern European

twang to his accent. A twang he never used to have. "You always thought you were funny."

"You used to always say I was funny."

"I was lying."

"I find that hard to believe," Dwayne said. "I'm positively hilarious."

Gary smirked. His eyes darted down to Nico, who lay stationary in the driver's seat beside Dwayne. "Shit. Our old boy's not looking too good."

"Gary, I appreciate we've got scores to settle right now. Really, I do. But Nico's not good. He's been bitten."

"Bitten?"

"Bitten by some psycho back where he was picking up the car. I think he's lost a lot of blood. And that's why he's…"

Shit. What the hell was he even talking about? This whole situation was surreal. Everything about it was just completely messed up. Something was going on outside the car. Those riots. And now a hold up of traffic. Something was going down.

And Nico. Nico right beside him. Unconscious? Dead? He didn't know. He didn't have a god damned clue.

He'd just robbed a frigging cash machine in a frigging bank. He had the cash on his lap. And an absolute lunatic was standing at the car window.

And somehow, he was still *joking* about shit.

"Look," Gary said. "I don't give a shit what you get up to in your free time. Whatever kinky shit you're into together, that ain't any of my business. The only business I'm interested in is sitting there on your lap."

Dwayne's stomach sank. The money. Of course he was here for the money. Of course he didn't give two shits about what was going on outside. If he was anything like Dwayne, this was more of a *distraction* to him than anything. An opportunity. A chance to strike when the city was in disarray—while the *country* was in disarray, by the sounds of things.

Dwayne cradled the cash. "Gary, today isn't the day for—"

"Today is exactly the day for this shit," Gary said. "So don't you try worming your way out of this right now."

"Nico. He needs help. And—"

Gary reached into his front jacket pocket and pulled out a pistol.

He tapped on the glass. Pointed it right through the window, right at Dwayne.

"Woah," Dwayne said, raising his hands.

"Cut the 'conscientious citizen' act right now. You don't give a shit about Nico. You don't give a shit about anyone other than yourself. And you're not as weak and submissive as you're making out right now. You're a predator. You and me, we ain't so different. Which means you already know how this is going to end."

Shit. Yeah. Dwayne wasn't fooling Gary. Gary knew him well. He could maybe buy himself a little bit of time with most people, enough time to *appear* vulnerable, and think things through. But Gary wasn't one of those people. Gary had seen him in action a ton of times already. So he wasn't falling for the act.

"Then you'll know why I can't hand over this cash," Dwayne said.

"But I'm standing here with a pistol. I don't think you're really in a position to be chatting back right now."

Dwayne looked over at Nico. Nico lay back against the car seat headrest. His eyes twitched. His mouth quivered at the sides. More blood trickled out, down his chin. Truth be told, he wasn't sad. He kind of liked Nico, in a superficial, don't get too attached to anyone way. But truthfully, as shitty as it may be, when he'd seen Nico pass out, he'd felt this twinge of possibility. An opportunity. An opportunity to take the money himself and run.

And when he got away, he'd keep a good chunk of that money, for...

"Hand over the cash."

"If I hand over the cash, I'm dead. Mobeen will kill me."

"That's not my problem."

"Come on, Gary."

Gary lifted the pistol higher. He shoved it in through the window, right towards Dwayne's head.

"Look at me," Gary said. "I'm holding a gun to your head in broad daylight. You're trapped in traffic. The police can't get here. *No one* can get here. And nobody gives a crap anyway. Because some shit is going down."

"Your point being?'

"If you hand that cash over... you've got a chance, buddy. A chance to get away. A chance to dash away from Mobeen before he has a chance to catch up with you."

"Without my cash."

Gary shrugged. "Take a couple of hundred."

"A couple of hundred?"

"Enough to get you a flight away from here."

"And after I get a flight away from here? Live as a homeless Spaniard?"

"The rest isn't my problem. I'm being generous here."

"Oh, truly. Your generosity knows no bounds."

Dwayne sat there in the passenger seat. The absurdity of the situation weighed down on his shoulders. Sitting here. Pistol to his head. Cash on his lap. Trapped in some kind of mass panic. And a possibly dead Nico beside him.

Shit. Was this what being truly desensitised really felt like? Being in this situation and not even feeling a glimmer of emotion other than... well, frustration?

"Hand it over," Gary said.

"You can't stand there pointing a gun to my head forever, Gary."

"No. No I can't. Which is why I'll pull this trigger if you don't hand it over."

"Gary—"

"You've got ten seconds," Gary shouted. "Ten seconds to hand it over. I've played nice. I've been more than generous. Now it's your turn to co-operate. 'Cause I'll shoot. Believe me, I'll shoot. What's it gonna be?"

Dwayne's heart started racing. His mouth dried up. Ten seconds. Ten seconds, to save himself. Ten seconds, to think this through.

He thought of Mum.

He thought of seeing her, tumbling out of that stairlift.

He thought of her cries, and her screams.

The way she held his hands.

"Please, Dwayne. Please don't leave me here."

He thought about her and he closed his eyes.

"Five seconds, Dwayne."

Dwayne swallowed a lump in his throat.

Five seconds.

Five seconds to save his life.

Five seconds to save—

"Don't do this, Dwayne. Don't do this."

He opened his eyes. The light from beyond the windscreen poured in. The cars stacked up. People running down the road, fear etched on their faces. He saw the panic. He saw the confusion.

And then he saw that opportunity.

Right there in the glove compartment.

The opportunity he'd spent the last few seconds trying to work towards.

Because Gary might know him well. But he clearly didn't know him well enough.

And that opportunity was a pistol of his own, in the rucksack.

He held the pistol in hand.

"Now, Dwayne. You'd better hand it over right now. Or—"

"Okay," Dwayne said. "Okay."

Gary's eyes narrowed. "What?"

"It's yours," Dwayne said.

He lifted the rucksack.

He waited until Gary was holding it. Until both his hands were occupied.

"Gary?" Dwayne said.

Gary nodded. "Huh?"

"I'm sorry."

And then he went to pull the trigger.

But before he did... something happened.

Something... something right beside him.

In the driver's seat, Nico's eyes rolled back into place.

He gasped. Blood spluttered right down his chin.

And then he let out a deafening shriek, and clamped his teeth around Gary's forearm.

PETE

* * *

Pete had seen some crazy shit in his fifteen years on the force.

He'd seen elderly women stabbing their abusive husbands. He'd seen kids living in unimaginable poverty and neglect. He'd seen overdoses. He'd seen the mashed remains of a suicide victim stretched across a railway line. He'd seen all sorts of shit.

But somehow, nothing matched the craziness of what he was staring at right now.

Colin's teeth were wedged right into Stan's face. His incisors clamped down on his cheeks. He was biting down—hard. Stan was screaming. Screaming like mad as blood drooled down his cheeks.

"Get off!" he wailed. "Get off! Get off!"

And Pete could only sit there. Sit there and stare as Colin bit down even harder. As he tore back his skin, ripped away the muscles on his face. Whatever drug he was on... Pete hadn't seen anything like it before. The violence, sure. But that *strength*...

Colin was a scrote. A weak, skinny scrote. So that *strength*. Where the hell had that come from? Especially when he'd looked so *incapacitated* moments earlier.

The smell of blood filled the police car. Blood. Blood, splattering everywhere. Splashing up on the windows. Spraying over the seats.

"Colin," Pete gasped. "Stop—stop—"

And he sounded so pathetic. He knew he sounded so pathetic. But this wasn't normal. This wasn't right. And all his instincts as a police officer, all his instincts about protecting other people—about protecting his *own*—all of that drifted away, and in its place: fear.

"Help!" Stan cried. "Help!"

"Colin," Pete muttered.

He grabbed Stan. Pulled him back with all his strength. Stan screamed. "No! No! No!" His face. As Pete pulled him back, the skin of his face started to tear away even more. Stan could see bone. Bone, staring out from underneath the torn flesh. Blood-smeared bone.

"Please!" Stan screamed. "Please!"

Blood splashed down onto Pete's hands. Colin held on to Stan's face. He wasn't letting go. Pulling him away was a bad idea, because the more he pulled, the more skin and flesh he tore away.

He needed to punch Colin off him.

He grabbed his truncheon. Whacked Colin across his head. "Colin. Get—get the hell off him. Right now."

But Colin didn't get off him. He didn't loosen his grip.

He kept clamped down on Stan's face. Like a dog, guarding its prey. One of the police dogs, holding the arms of the dog trainers. The more he struggled, the tighter he bit.

Pete smacked him again. Right on the middle of his head. "Colin," he gasped. But he didn't see much point. Colin wasn't here. Whatever drug-fuelled haze he was in, he certainly wasn't *here* right now.

And Colin wasn't letting go.

Pete pulled back that truncheon. In his mind's eye, Colin. That little shit. That little smirk on his face, whenever he pulled him up for anything. Petty crimes, usually. But this was different. The suspected murder. And... and...

Stan.

His face burned. His chest tightened. And this sense of *rage* took over him.

Colin.

Colin had been a problem for him for far too many years.

He swung that truncheon against his head—hard. Very damned hard.

Colin *should've* let go. That punch *should've* been enough to loosen his grip on his neck. It *should've* been enough to knock him out clean.

But Colin was still holding on.

Pete sat there. Frozen. Covered in blood. A scream echoed down the road. He looked outside the window. Saw a curly-haired woman covered in blood, running down the road. There was a gaping wound across her left shoulder, bleeding badly. Her eyes were bloodshot. And she had this predatory snarl etched across her face.

And then she saw a kid. A kid, sitting in the back of a Land Rover. Banging against the glass. Tears streamed down his face. His mouth widened. He looked over his shoulder. Behind him, movement. Another person, wrestling him away. Blood. And...

And then Pete looked back at Colin and Stan. Almost like he was witnessing everything from outside his body.

Colin had finally unclamped himself from Stan's face. That was the good news.

He was sitting at the back of the car. Holding a chunk of meat. And he was... His eyes. The whites of his eyes glared out into nothingness again. Blood oozed freely out of his mouth, but this blood looked *black* now, somehow.

Stan cried. He lifted his shaking hands up to what remained of his mashed-up face. Where his eyes once were, there were two dark, bloody holes. His nose dangled loosely from his face, from a small thread of skin. "Please," he whimpered. Shaking. "Please..."

Pete looked at Stan.

He looked outside. Drivers slammed against their horns. A white van whizzed past, crashing into a blue Mini. And in the distance, flames rose.

And then he looked back at Stan.

Stan stretched his shaking hands out towards Pete. "Help me," he whimpered. "Help me. Help—help me!"

Pete saw Helen.

He thought about her at home. Thought about her looking out the window and seeing the panic. The confusion. The violence. He thought about how he couldn't get hold of her. And he was worried about her.

Because whatever was happening here... it was happening everywhere.

"Help!" Stan shouted.

Pete grabbed the handle. He turned it. Opened the door. Then he clambered outside, tumbling to his arse, smacking his back against the warm concrete. The screaming grew louder now he was outside. The smell of smoke filled his lungs. Sirens and alarms rang out everywhere. Dogs barked, and people shouted.

"Please!" Stan gasped.

Pete stood. He held the door to the police car. Stan stared up at him with that bloody, mashed-up, Elephant Man-esque face.

And behind him... Colin grunted.

His eyes rolled back ahead.

He opened his mouth.

And Pete knew round two was about to begin.

"I'm sorry," he said. "I'm so sorry, buddy."

"No," Stan said. "No, don't—please. Please. Please!"

Pete slammed the police car door shut.

And then he locked it.

He heard Stan screaming. The car rocked forwards and backwards. He couldn't see properly through the blood-soaked windows, but he could hear shouting. Screaming. *Begging*.

His eyes clouded. A lump swelled in his throat. "I'm sorry. I'm —I'm truly sorry."

And he was. He really was.

But it was time to think of family now.

It was time to think of Helen now.

He turned around and went to run away, down the road, away from the chaos, when he saw something that made him freeze.

Three people.

Two men and a woman.

All of them covered in blood.

All of them with that same look of anger etched across their faces.

Standing there.

Standing there and staring at the empty space where Pete knew himself to be.

And then, after a moment's pause, they all lunged towards Pete.

DAVID

* * *

David heard the growl behind him and the hairs on the back of his neck stood right on end.

He saw the puddle of blood on the floor by the back door. He saw those faint footprints, walking their way into the kitchen. He saw the way they disappeared underneath him. Behind him.

And then he heard that growl.

It sounded like a dog. Like an angry, terrified dog, warding off an intruder. But there was something else about it. Something about its tone. Something distinctly... well, *human* about it.

David stared ahead into the utility room, and. A cold shiver crept down his spine. His heart pounded. A dizziness washed over him. That growl. That growl, right behind him.

And... Mrs Kirkham.

He'd seen her. Out in the garden. Standing there. Blood dripping down her face. Her grey hair laced with crimson. And that blank expression in her eyes. That *dead* expression in her eyes.

And then she'd started walking towards the house. Walking

towards the back door. She'd had an accident. That's all it was. She'd had some kind of accident, and she needed help. She was old. She was on her own. She'd had some kind of fall. That's all there was to it.

But that growl.

That growl didn't sound like someone who'd had any kind of accident.

David swallowed a lump in his throat.

He didn't want to turn around. But he knew he had to.

He took a breath of that clammy air. Smelled sour milk. Tasted rust. A metallic tang of rust, hanging in the air. And something like damp earth on a summer's day.

He had to turn around.

He had to look.

He had to...

And then he turned around.

Mrs Kirkham stood in front of him. Her long, grey hair dangled over her shoulders, speckled with blood. Her eyes stared ahead, to somewhere beyond David; to somewhere *behind* him, like he wasn't even there at all. Dark brown urine trickled down her leathery inner thigh. It didn't stop. Just leaked out of her, all over David's kitchen floor.

"Mrs—Mrs Kirkham," David said. "Are you okay?"

Stupid question. She was covered in blood and she was pissing all over David's kitchen floor. Of course she wasn't frigging okay. If anything, she was in an even worse state than he'd first feared.

Mrs Kirkham groaned. A bloody gargle filled the silence of the kitchen.

Crap. That sound. That sound wasn't... it wasn't human. It was unlike anything David had ever heard. What the hell was wrong with her? What the hell was going on?

"Mrs Kirkham," David said. His heart pounding. "Are... are you..."

Mrs Kirkham growled again. Louder, this time. She bore her

yellow, bloody teeth. There were chunks of something between her teeth.

Chunks of meat.

David felt sick. He didn't know what he was looking at. He didn't *understand* what had happened to Mrs Kirkham. But whatever'd happened, she was in a bad way. A really bad way.

He thought about the news. The attack at the hospital. The attacks at hospitals across the country. And then the riots. The inner city riots.

He looked at Mrs Kirkham and he wondered. Even though it didn't add up, even though it didn't make sense... he wondered.

Was this related, somehow?

Because this wasn't right. This wasn't just an old woman who'd had a fall.

This was a woman who'd suffered.

A woman who'd suffered something violent.

"Who did this?" David said. "What happened? What..."

And then Mrs Kirkham walked towards him.

She walked slowly. Lifted her shaking right foot, and then followed it with her left. She looked like she was learning to walk for the first time. Like a newborn deer, uneven, unsteady. But there was no doubt about where she was heading.

"Mrs Kirkham," David said. He stepped back a little. His heart rate picked up. His face burned hot. His throat wobbled. "What's—"

And then Mrs Kirkham's neck tilted to one side. David heard a crack. A splitting crack, as she bent her neck parallel with her shoulder, and then swung it back around again, upright.

And then she stared right into David's eyes.

She didn't budge. She didn't growl. Come to think of it... was she even *breathing*?

"Mrs Kirkham," David said. "Are you..."

And then Mrs Kirkham leapt towards David.

He staggered to his right. Threw himself over towards the

window. Splitting pain climbed up the right side of his body. What the hell? What was wrong with her? And that strength. Where the *hell* had that sudden strength and energy come from? She was an old woman. She wasn't supposed to move like that.

David turned around.

Mrs Kirkham lay on the kitchen floor. Her frail left arm was clearly broken on impact. Snapped, right in the middle of her forearm.

But Mrs Kirkham didn't show any signs of being in pain.

Come to think of it, she didn't show any signs of being affected by the attack... well, at *all*.

She crouched down on the floor, on all fours. Blood oozed from her nostrils. And her glazed eyes twitched, like she was blind, searching for David.

"Mrs Kirkham," David said. It was all he could say. "You need to..."

And then she clambered across the floor on all fours, like a spider, hurtling towards David.

David jumped up.

He swung across the kitchen worktop. He landed on his feet —remarkably—at the other side of the worktop. He ran into the utility room. Grabbed the kitchen door. Turned back around, towards Mrs Kirkham.

She lay flat on the floor. Blood trickled out of her forehead. Her neck was twisted, and looked... broken.

But her lips were still moving.

He didn't want to leave this woman. She needed help. Serious help.

But at the same time... something was wrong with her.

Really wrong with her.

That blood on her lips.

That meat between her teeth.

He couldn't put his finger on it. It was probably very primal.

But he couldn't shake a sense of fear.

Mrs Kirkham dragged herself around. Pushed herself up to her feet, still showing no signs of pain. No sign of giving up.

"I'm sorry," David said. "I'll come back. I'll make sure I see to you. But..."

She ran at him.

He slammed the back door.

Stepped outside.

Walked backwards, into his garden, almost losing his footing on the grass.

He looked back towards that back door as he stood outside in the heat. He heard her banging at the back door.

He had to get out of here. He had to get away. Keira. Keira was at the hospital. He didn't have his mobile. He didn't have his rucksack. Shit. He didn't have *anything*.

And he wasn't going back in there to get them.

He had to get to the hospital. Get around the front of the house then get in his car and get the hell out of here. That's it. That's what he had to do. He couldn't think too much about it. He couldn't overthink about it. He just had to do it.

He went to walk across the grass, staring intently at the back door, banging on its hinges, when he heard something that made another shiver creep right down his spine.

Another growl.

In the grass.

Right behind him.

KEIRA

* * *

Keira leaned back against the door and squeezed her eyes shut.

Screams filled the hospital corridors behind her. Alarms rang out all over the place. Her head was going to explode. The blood. The blood. The screaming. The fighting. The...

Gavin.

She saw him lying in front of her in the corridor, like she was experiencing it again. She saw Omar, straddling him. She saw him digging his long fingernails into Omar's stomach. Tearing his skin and his flesh away. She saw his intestines, spilling out like tinned spaghetti, all over the white hospital floor.

But it was Gavin's screams that replayed in her mind, again and again.

Like something out of a nightmare. Only... no, worse. Far, far worse. Because those screams were real. Those screams were the sound of a man suffering the worst agony.

And what had she done?

She'd turned around, slammed the door shut, and now here she was.

She realised her eyes weren't closed anymore. They were open. Open wide. The lights in this corridor had gone out. Walls that used to feel so comforting to her, so familiar to her, now felt alien. Barren. Dangerous. She looked down at her hands. They were shaking. Covered in blood.

Omar's blood.

Gavin's blood.

Blackpool...

No. No, she didn't want to think of Blackpool. She couldn't *afford* to think of Blackpool. Not right now.

Those alarm sirens echoed all around her. Those screams—real and imagined—replayed again and again in her mind. The rusty metallic tang of hot blood terrorised her nostrils. Burning, acidic vomit crept up her throat, threatening to spill out onto the floor around her.

She didn't know what to do. She was a nurse. She was a nurse and she was supposed to look after people. She was supposed to protect people. To care for people. And then she'd just watched someone... *die*? He must've died. There was no way Gavin was surviving that attack. There's no way *anyone* would survive an attack like that.

Omar. The way he'd passed out in front of her. Then the way he'd surfaced back to life, just like that. And with more energy than before. Way, way more energy than anyone bleeding out should be capable of.

His throat. The state of his throat. His arteries spewing blood. His vocal cords, severed, gnawed.

And yet he had the strength in him to stand right up? To attack Gavin? To wrestle him to the ground and do... well, to do *that?*

No. No that wasn't possible. Omar looked on death's door. And then to do what he'd done...

How was it possible?

She reached into her pocket. Pulled out her phone. Tried to load up the internet for some kind of news. Some kind of external input on what the hell was going on beyond a vague "attack" story. But nothing was loading. Shit. The internet wasn't working, and she had barely any signal.

She thought about who she could call. 999? What use was 999 when you were in a hospital, and when that hospital was spiralling out of control? She had no boyfriend. No partner. No Mum. And...

Dad. She pictured him the last time she saw him. "You'll call me, won't you?"

She remembered nodding. Remembered turning around, stepping out the door, eyes fuzzy with tears. Because she knew she was lying. She wouldn't be calling him. Not after that day.

She thought about friends. Best friends. Lydia, and Emily. People she used to go to the pub with on a Friday night. Barry. Steph. All of them, she'd drifted from. She kept in touch with none of them anymore. What was she supposed to do? What was she supposed to *say*?

No, she was alone. She was very much alone.

This was her bed. She'd made it.

Now she had to lie in it.

And by lying in it, she had to get the hell up and she had to do something.

She thought about Dad again. She couldn't call him because she didn't have his number anymore. She'd deleted it, and then she'd changed her own number and she'd made sure not to add it to her new phone. And even if she *could* get in touch with him... what use was he going to be right now? He'd never been there for her. He'd never looked out for her. What was going to change now?

But all the same, she needed to do something. She couldn't just sit here. She didn't know what the hell was going on behind those doors. But as she crouched against it, she saw herself, almost as if from outside her body. She was a nurse. And it was her duty to look after people. To protect them. To care for them.

And that's what she had to do.

And then she thought of Blackpool.

She saw the blood again.

She saw those pained, wide eyes.

She felt that hand holding hers.

"Please... please..."

And then she heard Gavin's screams and—

No.

She needed to get up.

She needed to be strong.

She needed to be a nurse.

She took a deep breath of the humid air. Her heart raced at a million beats per second. She felt dizzy. Faint. Like she was about to pass out at any given second.

But no. She wasn't going to pass out. Because this was her duty. This was her job.

She had people she cared about here. Colleagues. Friends. And she had people she cared *for* here, too.

She wasn't just walking away from them.

She wasn't just abandoning them.

She reached for the handle.

Lowered it.

The door didn't budge.

She frowned. Tried the door again. And again, no luck.

"What..."

And that's when it hit her.

That's when it crystallised, in her mind.

The door.

The door she'd run through in a desperate attempt to escape.

The door leading to the corridor that led to...

"The mortuary," she muttered.

She remembered the hysteria. The talk of someone called Hailee being attacked by a patient. And then her attacking Omar, and the pair of them going missing.

She remembered that talk, and she felt a stabbing sensation, right in the middle of her chest.

The mortuary door. Locked.

Two more *attackers* down here.

And then she heard something that made her world open up, right beneath her feet.

Behind her, somewhere down the long, narrow hospital corridor, Keira heard something that sent a shiver down her spine.

Footsteps.

NISHA

* * *

Nisha opened her mouth and gasped when the pressure pressed against her arm—the warm pressure of someone's hand.

Mrs Thompson. Pushing her back against the bathroom wall. Snarling at her with those shiny white teeth. Blood dripping down her face. She was here. She was here, and she was going to hurt her, and she was going to kill her, and—

She turned around.

The first thing Nisha noticed? It wasn't Mrs Thompson standing opposite her.

It was another kid. Beth. That was her name. Nisha didn't know her too well. She was in one of the other classes. Year Three, maybe. She saw other kids teasing Beth sometimes. Stealing glitter pens from her pencil case. She saw Beth crying, sometimes. Sitting on her own against the school wall outside and crying. She wanted to go over to Beth sometimes. She wanted to tell her she was going to be okay. That everything was going to be okay.

But... Beth stood in front of her. Her eyes bulged wide. Her cheeks glistened with tears. Her lips quivered. She raised a shaking finger to her mouth. Quiet. That's what that meant. The universal symbol for quiet.

And there was something else about Beth, too. Something else that Nisha noticed about her. There was something on her face. Specks of something, all over her face.

Specks of... Was that *blood*?

Beth pressed her finger hard against her lips. Damn. Why couldn't she hear? Because that look on Beth's face. How scared she looked. And that blood. Something had happened. Was it something to do with Mrs Thompson? Or was it something else?

And then Nisha saw them. Over by the door. Shadows. Shadows, creeping along, creeping past the classroom door. They weren't moving quickly. They were moving... slowly. Very slowly. Was it Mrs Thompson? Or was it somebody else? And why was Beth trying to keep her in here? Keep her quiet?

Mrs Thompson.

Those empty eyes.

That angry face.

And now this.

What was happening?

Nisha stared at Beth. Beth stared back at her. Tears crept down her cheeks. Nisha's heart raced. Just breathe. That's it. In. Out. In. Out. Just keep breathing. Just keep looking at Beth. Everything's going to be okay. Everything's going to be...

And then Beth turned around. Looked over at the door. The shadows were gone now. What was happening? What was going on?

And then Beth dragged her towards the door. Started running and dragging her towards the door. Was this a good idea? She wanted to ask her. But how could she ask her? Beth didn't understand sign. And Nisha wasn't even sure she *could* sign right now. Butterflies fluttered around her belly. Her knees wobbled like that jelly Dad made at weekends. She loved that jelly. She missed Dad. She wished Dad were here right now. Dad would know what to do.

Beth dragged her towards the door. No. No, she couldn't go out that door. Those shadows. That blood. And Mrs Thompson. She couldn't go out there. It was dangerous out there.

Beth's lips moved. She was saying something to Nisha. She was saying something to Nisha, but no sound was coming out. Or maybe it was. Nisha didn't know. But Nisha tried to read her lips. She tried to see what she was saying. But she couldn't tell. She just couldn't tell.

And then...

Beth lifted her hands.

At first, Nisha thought she was taking the mickey out of her. But no. This wasn't like when the other kids took the mickey out of her. Her hands. She was—she was trying to sign. She was...

Quiet now.

Safe now.

Go now.

The butterflies in her stomach stopped flapping. A warmth filled her body, like a hot bath on a cold day. Her eyes stung, and went all blurry. Beth could sign. Not very well. Kind of like how Nisha imagined people speaking different languages to sound when they were trying to speak English. That was all she had to compare it to.

But suddenly she didn't feel so alone.

Suddenly, she didn't feel quite as scared.

Beth reached for the door. She grabbed the handle. Waited there a few seconds. She narrowed her eyes. Pressed her ear to the door. Waited. Waited for *forever*.

And then she nodded, and she opened the door.

She rushed out, holding Nisha's hand. Nisha followed her out into the corridor. It was quiet. Empty. And it felt like there were scary monsters hiding around every corner. It used to feel safe. At first, when she first came here, it was scary. Because there were people behind every door. And sometimes she didn't see them, and they banged into her, and didn't help her up.

But she felt better as time went on. She felt *safer* as time went on.

But now, she didn't feel safe at all.

She looked over at the toilets. There was nobody there. No sign of Mrs Thompson. No one. Was that a good thing or a bad thing? She didn't know.

Beth yanked her arm, pulling her down the corridor, down towards the corner that led to the main hall, where they had P.E. and did assembly every Monday and Wednesday. She reached the end of the corridor, right to the end, when suddenly she stopped.

Her eyes widened. She put her finger to her lips again. Stood there. Still. Very still.

Nisha's heart raced. Dizziness took over her. There was someone here. There was someone close by. She could *smell* them. The smell of metal. The smell of wet mud on a sunny day. The smell of...

And then she turned to the classroom door beside her. Year Two. The door was open a little bit. It was closed before, but it was open now.

And there were footprints.

Bloody footprints in front of that door.

Little dirty puddles of blood.

Nisha walked over to that door. Slowly. Her heart beat faster. She wasn't sure what she was going to find. She wasn't sure she *wanted* to find whatever was in there.

She reached the door. Looked around at Beth, who still had her finger to her mouth, who glared at Nisha.

And then she turned back to the door.

She took another step towards it.

Don't look.

Don't look.

Don't...

And then she peeked around the corner.

Bright sunshine beamed in through the windows. The air was warm, stuffy. Nisha always liked Year Two class. She liked the pictures on the walls. The pictures from cartoons. Bugs Bunny. Roadrunner. Tom and Jerry. All her favourites. You didn't need interpreters to find those cartoons funny.

But right now those cartoon pictures were covered in blood.

And in the middle of the classroom, on the floor...

Kids.

She thought they were just playing some game at first. It was a joke. It was all some big joke at her expense. They were all going to jump up and they were all going to laugh at her and she was going to feel her face burn and her eyes sting, all over again.

But that blood.

And...

A little boy lay on his side. There was a chunk of meat missing from his neck.

A little girl lay on her back. Her face was completely red. It looked like it'd been chewed at. Her blue summer dress was red, like she'd had an accident with the paint set.

Dizziness swallowed Nisha. Her face burned. A burning feeling rose up her throat, into her mouth.

She needed to get away.

She needed to stop looking.

She needed to stop looking at the bodies.

At the flies.

At the blood.

She needed to—

Something covered her mouth. Tasted salty. A hand.

She shook side to side. Grabbed the hand. Pulled it away. And then she turned around.

She expected to see Beth standing there. Finger to her lips again.

But... Beth wasn't facing her.

Beth stared off down the corridor, where they'd both come from.

At the end of that corridor...

Mrs Thompson.

The head teacher, Mr Rawford.

And one of the dinner ladies. Mrs Potstello.

All of them stood there.

All of them stared at her.

All of them had splashes of blood on their clothes.

All of them had... pieces of meat missing from their body.

And all of them had this *dead* look to their eyes.

Her heart raced. Her mouth went dry.

The kids.

The kids in Year Two.

The kids in the classroom.

Her and Beth needed to get away.

Her and Beth needed to—

And then, just like that, the three grown-ups ran towards her and Beth.

DWAYNE

* * *

Dwayne sat in the passenger seat of Nico's hire car and he tried to wrap his head around what in the name of God he was looking at.

Nico... Nico clamped his teeth around Gary's bicep. He was biting down on it so hard that blood was gushing out of it.

And Dwayne could only think of what Nico had told him earlier.

The wanker who'd bitten him. The wanker who'd bitten him back at the car hire place. And now *he* was biting someone else?

What the hell was going on?

Gary screamed like a little girl. A blast tore through the car. An explosion filled Dwayne's head. His ears rang like mad. What the hell was that noise?

And then he saw it. The pistol. The pistol in Gary's hand.

And then the smashed glass, right by Dwayne's side. He'd pulled that trigger. He'd almost taken Dwayne's frigging head off in the process.

Gary screamed even louder. He tried to yank his arm away, but Nico just clamped down even harder. Blood gushed all over the car. His screams cut through the ringing in Dwayne's ears.

And Nico's *eyes*.

That look in his damned eyes.

His eyes looked... filled with blood. That was it. Like someone had turned a bloody tap on and filled them with blood. He'd never seen Nico like this before. He had a temper sometimes, sure. But never like this.

This was way beyond anything he'd ever seen from Nico before.

Or anything he'd ever seen from *anyone* before.

He saw the rucksack on Nico's lap now. And that pistol. It fell from Gary's hand and landed in the glove compartment. And Dwayne could only sit there, holding his own pistol. He could only sit there, frozen, watching the chaos unfold before him.

He didn't want to help Gary. Gary was a prick. He'd just almost shot him. He wouldn't hesitate about putting a bullet through his head. Dwayne was sure of it.

But Nico.

He liked Nico. Got on well with him. Wouldn't exactly call him a "friend," but he got on with him a lot better than most people he'd been forced to work with over the years. They weren't exactly similar. Nico was a massive hedonist, and paranoid beyond all rationality. Loved his conspiracy theories to a terrifying degree.

But... right now, Dwayne saw something opening up in front of him. He saw an opportunity. He saw... a chance.

A chance to grab that rucksack.

A chance to grab that cash.

And a chance to get away.

Gary's blood splattered against his face. Gary punched at Nico now. Punched at his head, trying to swat him away, trying to break free.

But Nico just wasn't letting go.

Dwayne looked at that cash on Nico's lap. And then he looked out the car's rear window. Gary's bike. The traffic was bad, but if he could get on Gary's bike… he could get the hell out of here. He could get the hell to the airport. And he could get that cash where it needed to go.

He thought about the Spanish sun. He thought about Mum.

He thought about the lengths he'd go to, for family.

"I'm sorry," he said.

And then he grabbed the rucksack off Nico's lap and pulled the passenger door handle.

The door didn't open.

"Shit." Why wasn't it opening? Was it *jammed*? Shit. This wasn't right. What the hell was happening?

He yanked the handle again. Tried to turn it. Tried to open it.

But the door wasn't budging.

He was locked in.

He was trapped in here.

"Jesus, Nico. Was now really the time for a child lock?"

He turned around and he saw something… different.

Gary was still screaming. That much was true.

But… he wasn't in the car. Not anymore.

He was outside the window. Leaning forward. Holding on to his arm and screaming into space.

And Nico…

Nico wasn't holding on to him anymore.

He wasn't biting him.

He was…

Looking right at Dwayne.

Or rather, right *through* Dwayne.

His eyes looked grey and dead. His mouth twitched. Bloody chunks of flesh trickled down his face.

"Nico?" he said.

Nico's head twitched. For a moment, for just a flash, a glimmer of recognition flickered in Nico's eyes.

"It's me," Dwayne said. Mouth dry. Heart pounding. "We—we got the money. Now we've got to go. We've..."

And before he could say another word, Nico lunged towards him.

PETE

* * *

Pete stood in the middle of the traffic-filled road and watched the bloody mob of three hurtle towards him.

He spun around and he ran. Shit. Shit, shit, shit. He'd seen what Colin had done to Stan, back in the police car. The way he'd sunk his teeth into his face. Torn it away. And it had to be a coincidence, right? Colin was just high. He was tripping off his face—no pun intended—and he'd attacked Stan violently as a result.

But... the news from the station. The attack. And then the scenes all around him. The woman running between the cars. The man launching onto her, pinning her down, screaming. All the riots and all the violence across the country. He didn't understand it. He didn't know what in God's name was going on.

But he knew one damned thing for sure.

Something was happening.

Something *big*.

He raced down the road as fast as he bloody well could. He needed to step up. He needed to be a man. No. Not *just* a man.

He needed to be a police officer. He was supposed to be about law. About order. About protecting people in need.

But... Helen.

She was back home. He couldn't get hold of her. And with everything going on down here on the streets—with all the confusion, all the panic—he was worried. Because if Helen wasn't answering, then she might be in danger.

Big danger.

A chorus of gargled cries erupted right behind Pete. He spun around. The three people—two men and a woman—hurtled after him. All of them were covered in blood. And all of them had this dead-eyed gaze.

A dead-eyed gaze that reminded him of Colin.

He spun back round. Tried to run faster. Come on. He was faster than this. He'd put a bit of a belly on in recent years—a belly Helen kept urging him to go to the gym and lose—but it wasn't enough of a belly to slow him down *this* much.

The trio growled. Somewhere in the maze of traffic, a man screamed. "Help me! Not my boy! Please not my boy!"

Pete tried to block it out. He had to run. He had to keep going. He didn't know where he was going right now. Just that he had to keep going. He had to keep moving. He had to get away. He couldn't let them—

Something solid slammed against his right foot. He tumbled forward, through the air, in slow motion. Shit. Shit, shit, shit. He couldn't fall. He had to stay on his feet. He had to—

The road slammed against his face. The rusty taste of blood filled his mouth. A splitting pain burst across his head.

But more than anything... that fear.

He was on the road.

He was on the road and the group were almost onto him and—

He dragged himself up to his feet.

A hand snatched at his wrist. Yanked it back, almost pulling him back to the road.

One of the group. The woman. Sinking her purple-polished nails into his skin. She looked young. Couldn't be older than late teens. Pretty. Reminded him of...

No. No, don't go there, Pete. Not now.

But right now, she looked... possessed. That was his only damned word for it. Possessed.

She dragged her mouth towards his arm.

Pete pulled back his truncheon and he cracked her across the head.

Hard.

She let go of his arm. But the other two. They were close.

And...

Off in the distance, more figures raced between the cars. They all had this same glimmer of violence in their eyes. Kind of like people off their faces on spice. Or on a bad trip. Pete had seen it more than enough times on the job. People off their faces, losing control.

But this...

There were so many of them. And this went beyond a mere drugs episode. Some of these people were just kids. And some were older, too. Not that kids and old people never took drugs.

But one of the men was a businessman in a suit wearing a gold Rolex. The other, a bloke who had to be in his eighties, wearing a T-shirt that read "Man at Work" with a picture of a barbecue in the middle. They weren't the type. They just weren't the type. There was no other way of putting it.

They were normal people.

And yet...

He swung the truncheon against the girl's head again. Winced when it made contact. He didn't want to hurt her. But at the same time... she wanted to hurt him.

He went to stagger back when he heard something by his side.

The car. The car next to him. A girl sat inside. Little girl. Couldn't be much older than high school years.

Tears streamed down her cheeks. Mascara stained her skin. "Please," she cried. "Please."

Pete heard the growling opposite.

He turned around. Saw them hurtling at him. The businessman. The other bloke. And the girl. The girl whose head he'd just fucking *cracked*.

And out of pure instinct… Pete thought of Helen.

He thought of Helen and he thought of their girl, their Sarah, and how old she'd be right now—how she'd be at high school right now, how she should be here, and how…

Another growl.

A cry.

And that girl. That girl in the car. That girl who needed help.

"Please," she gasped.

Pete thought of Helen, and he looked at the mob surging his way.

And then he grabbed the car door handle.

Opened it.

And then he turned around and he started to run.

He saw the mob turn their attention from him to the open door of the car.

He saw them look inside.

And then he turned around, and he bit his lip, and he swallowed a lump in his throat.

"I'm sorry," he gasped. "I'm sorry."

It was a few more seconds before he heard the sound that would forever haunt his nightmares.

The girl's agonised scream.

DAVID

* * *

David heard growling, right behind him.

He stood in the middle of his back garden, shaking. He couldn't stop shaking. Mrs Kirkham. The way she'd attacked him. The way she'd hurled herself across the kitchen at him. The way she'd snapped her arm, and shown no signs of pain at all. It wasn't right. It was like a nightmare. Like a God damned nightmare.

And yet... David was pretty sure this wasn't a dream.

That growling. Right behind him. He didn't want to turn around. He didn't want to see *whatever* it was. Because he couldn't shake the feeling that something had *done* something to Mrs Kirkham. Something must've happened to her to make her like that. And judging by that growling right behind him... he couldn't help feeling like that might be the source.

He didn't want to turn around. He didn't want to look over his shoulder. He just stood there. Heart racing. Staring at the back door of his house, rattling on its hinges. Splitting, agonised cries from inside. Mrs Kirkham. Showing a strength he didn't know she had—no, a strength he was *certain* she didn't have. 'Cause no old woman was that strong. Hell, no old man was that strong. And truth be told, take age out of the equation entirely. No one was that strong. Especially with the sorts of injuries they had.

But that growling.

Right behind him.

He closed his burning eyes. That blanket of darkness was comforting—for a moment. He took a deep breath of the warm, clammy summer air. In the distance, sirens echoed. The faint smell of burning filled his nostrils. Dizziness crept up on him. Colours filled his vision.

Keira.

Keira was in danger.

He needed to get down to the hospital and he needed to find her.

He needed…

Another growl.

He opened his eyes. Swallowed a lump in his throat.

He didn't know what he would find when he turned around. He didn't know who—or what—he was going to see.

But whatever it was… he couldn't hide away from it forever.

He needed to know. Because if this was all linked, and if whatever affliction Mrs Kirkham had succumbed to was the same damned affliction ripping through the hospitals right now—then he was in danger. Until the police got control of the situation, *everyone* was in danger.

He turned around.

Slowly.

A part of him not wanting to look.

A part of him not wanting to see.

A part of him not wanting to know.

When he turned around… he didn't see anything.

Grass. Tall, overgrown grass, which was long overdue for a chop.

And in the middle of that grass...

The growling. That's where it was. In the middle of that tall grass.

Someone was in there.

David's skin crawled. His throat tightened. His heart raced faster, a feat he barely believed possible, since it was already going way faster than it should be. End up having a heart attack at this rate. Needed to change his focus. Needed to stop thinking about it. But shit, trying *not* to think about it just made his heart race a whole lot frigging faster.

He soon had the distraction he needed.

Eyes.

A pair of eyes. Right in the middle of that tall grass. Staring up at him.

Crap. Someone was there. Someone was watching him. Like a lion, sitting in the grass, eyeing up its prey.

He needed to get the hell out of here.

He needed to run.

He needed to...

Those eyes moved.

The figure in the grass shifted, edging closer towards him.

David turned back towards the house. But the back door was still rattling on its hinges. Mrs Kirkham was still in there. Trying to get out.

He looked at the fence beside him. Blood dripped down it. Shit. Mrs Kirkham must've climbed over it. The old woman must've climbed over it and fallen into his garden and...

Shit, he didn't have time to think about the ins and outs of it right now.

He had to get out of this garden.

He ran towards the fence.

Reached for the top of it to hurl himself over.

Something growled beside him, and then...

Wait.

Was that...

He held the fence. Shaking.

He turned around. Slowly.

And he looked into the figure's eyes.

It wasn't a person. And it wasn't someone who had it in for him at all, by the looks of things.

It was a dog.

Long golden hair. Big black eyes. Panting. Saliva drooling down the sides of its mouth.

"What..."

And then he saw the patch on its back.

The bloody patch.

The teeth marks.

"Oh no," David said.

The dog growled. Wagged its tail. He didn't recognise the dog. Didn't know where it'd come from. But it was here in his garden. And it looked like it'd been... bitten? Crap. What the hell was happening? It didn't make sense. None of it made sense.

He looked at that dog and he felt a wave of sadness. Him and Rina always wanted a dog. Said they'd wait until Keira got older before adopting one from a rescue shelter. But life got in the way, as it always did. Bills stacked up. Time disintegrated. And before they knew it, the moment had passed, and their marriage had gone stale, and...

The screeching of tires.

The gasps outside.

The scream.

David swallowed a lump in his throat.

The dog growled. Then it barked. It had a collar draped around its neck. A name tag dangled down from it. It had its balls, so it was a "he."

And even though instinct told him to turn away, even though instinct told him to run... he heard that banging kitchen door, and heard the sirens, and smelled the smoke, and he couldn't bring himself to leave this dog behind right now.

"Come on, lad," he said, walking over towards it. "We're gonna be okay, me and you. We're gonna be..."

That's when he heard it.

The kitchen door.

Creaking.

Creaking in the way it did when it was being...

Opened.

He turned around. Dreading what he was about to find. But knowing, deep down, exactly what he was going to see.

Who he was going to see.

His stomach sank.

Mrs Kirkham was in the garden.

And she was racing right towards him.

KEIRA

* * *

Keira heard the footsteps pounding down the corridor and her entire body went numb.

She stared at the door, back towards the ward she'd just fled. Behind that door, she heard screaming. Shouting. Alarms blaring. The sound of trolleys tumbling over. Of patients begging for their lives.

"Please! No! Please!"

And behind her... those footsteps.

Getting closer.

Echoing down the corridor.

Her heart raced. She had to get out of here. But where the hell was she going to go? She couldn't go back on the ward. She'd already seen the panic out there. She wasn't exactly going to go back there right after she'd just got away, was she?

Omar.

Omar, straddling Gavin.

Dragging his belly open.

Blood spilling everywhere.

Intestines pooling out like spaghetti in sauce from a tin.

And Gavin's pig-like squeals.

She felt sick. Dizzy. Ringing filled her ears. She couldn't take this. She couldn't cope. She couldn't do this. She couldn't...

Breathe. Just breathe.

She took a deep breath in. The air was cool in here, and musty. She held it there. Held it for what felt like forever, but was probably just a few seconds.

And then she released it.

In again.

Out again.

And then she turned around.

The corridor was empty.

She couldn't hear those footsteps anymore.

Just the buzzing of the flickering lights above. The shouting in the rest of the hospital. The alarms ringing out, blaring. And distant sirens from far beyond these walls.

But no footsteps.

She looked down the long, dark corridor. It looked longer than ever before, stretching off into the distance. She saw the sign up ahead. The sign, pointing off to the left.

MORTUARY.

And she remembered what Jean told her. An incident. An incident, down here in the mortuary. This was where Omar was attacked. Attacked by a woman who'd been attacked by someone else.

And where were those attackers?

Both missing.

She stared down the corridor. Saw the double doors in the distance. If she could make it to those double doors, she could get out of here. She could push through those doors, run to the staircase, and then she could run out of the emergency exit and leave this place behind.

But then...

She was a nurse. She had a duty to her patients. And a duty to her friends here, too. Friends like Jean.

She thought about Gavin. The way she'd left him lying there, begging for his life. Could she have done more to help him? Because she was a nurse. She was supposed to care for other people. She'd failed to care for him. And what did that say about her?

She was afraid.

That's what it said about her.

She was afraid.

She looked down the corridor. The lights on the ceiling flickered. Those double doors stared back at her, taunting her, inviting her, so near yet so far.

She had to get out of here.

She didn't have a choice.

She walked. Walked down the corridor. Focused on the doors. If she didn't look over her shoulder or in any direction at all, she could convince herself everything was okay. Just a normal walk down a hospital corridor. That's all it was. A normal walk down a hospital corridor, just like she did every single day.

She walked quicker. She glanced up at the Mortuary sign. An arrow pointed left, down towards the mortuary area. She didn't want to look down there. She didn't want to see what was down there.

She looked back at those double doors ahead of her and behind the glass, she saw something move.

She froze.

A dark shadow. That's all it looked like. A smudge, drifting past, catching her eye.

Her stomach turned. She couldn't breathe. She couldn't breathe. She wasn't alone in here. There was someone else down here. There was someone else down here, and they were going to drag her to the floor like Omar did, and then they were going to rip her belly open, and...

No.

No. That wasn't happening. She needed to stay alive.

Because the hospital needed her.

She lifted a foot.

To her left, she heard another shuffling sound.

She stopped. Froze. Was that movement? Or was it in her head?

She didn't want to turn around. Didn't want to look down the corridor. Didn't want to see.

And then she heard another footstep.

And a growl.

Colours filled her vision. Her heartbeat raced. Blood whooshed through her skull.

That growl.

Someone was here.

Someone was in this section of the hospital with her.

She didn't want to turn around. She didn't want to look down the corridor. Because at the moment, by *not* seeing what was growling at her, in a way it shielded the reality from her. In a way, it made it... less real.

But she knew what she had to do.

Shaking, she turned her neck.

Slowly.

A woman stood in the middle of the corridor.

She was standing still. Very still. It was hard to make out her features, mostly because the light above her was flickering.

But Keira could see one thing very clearly.

She was covered in blood.

Blood ran down her chin. It was smeared across her neck. And it was splattered all the way down her blue hospital scrubs.

She stared at Keira. Or rather... it felt like she was staring *through* her. Like she was aware that *something* was standing right here, but didn't recognise it as Keira, somehow. Didn't recognise it as... well, as another *person,* somehow.

Just like Omar.

Her heart raced. Her feet felt like they'd been dipped in concrete. A warmth spread across her thighs, and she realised she was pissing herself.

"What..." she whimpered.

And that's when a bang echoed through the corridor.

She turned around.

It was the door back to the ward.

It was open.

And...

Gavin was racing through it.

His intestines trailing along beside him.

And behind him, Omar.

And both of them were coming for her.

Both of them were—

That's when the woman in front of her let out a piercing shriek, and then flew down the corridor towards her.

NISHA

* * *

Nisha saw Mrs Thompson, Mr Rawford and the dinner lady, Mrs Potstello, running down the corridor towards her and Beth, and she felt like she was in a bad dream.

They all ran towards her and Beth. Mrs Thompson snarled, opening her mouth like she was letting out a loud cry. Blood splattered from Mr Rawford's lips as he ran down the corridor like an out-of-control lion. And Mrs Potstello... the last thing Nisha heard, she had cancer. She wasn't supposed to be able to run like this. She'd lost all her hair and got really sick and they had a nice assembly for her where they all clapped and all made her nice things even though nobody really liked her 'cause she was mean and always gave Nisha ham even though she wasn't meant to eat ham.

But she looked sick in a different way now.

Even sicker.

But moving.

Fast.

She grabbed Beth's hand and she pulled her down the corridor, away from the three grown ups.

She turned the corner, towards the sports hall.

The caretaker barged through the doors. His cracked glasses dangled off his nose. The bottom half of his face looked like it'd been ripped away. And he was running towards them. Fast.

Nisha looked back at the teachers.

Then at the caretaker.

And then she looked at the door to her right and she knew there was only one place she could go.

The place she didn't want to go.

She dragged Beth inside the Year Two classroom where she'd seen the horrible things.

She turned around when she dragged Beth inside. She pushed the door shut.

But Mr Rawcliffe slammed against the door. Pushed against it. Hard.

Nisha pressed up against the door. She wasn't strong enough. She was weak, and she was little, and she wasn't going to be able to stop them getting through.

She looked around.

Beth stood there. Her mouth dangled wide open. Tears rolled down her cheeks. She was looking around the classroom.

Looking at the dead kids.

Looking at the blood.

Looking at the guts.

Looking at—

And then she looked back up at Nisha. Moved her lips. But Nisha couldn't understand her. She couldn't hear her properly.

Nisha pressed against the door with her body and she lifted her hands.

Window.

Beth shook her head.

The door bashed open.

Mr Rawcliffe grabbed Nisha.

Nisha cried and she pointed, pointed at the window.

And Beth looked at her, screaming, shouting, moving her mouth and crying and then she looked across the classroom and over at the window.

She ran over to it. Ran over to it. Tried to open it. But it wasn't budging. That's what Nisha could see her trying to say. It wasn't budging, and she was turning around and trying to say more things to Nisha, but Nisha couldn't hear her, she couldn't hear what she was trying to say, she could…

And then she saw the chair beside the window and she saw the window smashing and—and yes, that's what she had to do, that's exactly what she had to do.

So she ran.

She ran and she knew they were behind her, she knew they were chasing her, she could see the chair by the window and she could see herself smashing it and—

And then something grabbed her ankle.

She fell over. Smacked the floor. Or, no. She smacked into something squishy. Something…

She saw eyes staring up at her.

Dead eyes.

She jumped back. Ginger Harry. Lying dead on the floor. His face all pale. Blood all over his throat.

And she felt so bad for him. 'Cause he got bullied enough already. Bullied, and then hurt like this—killed like this.

This was a nightmare. This was a bad dream. This was…

And that's when Harry's eyes twitched.

His mouth twitched at the corners.

He stretched out a hand, and he moved that thick, purple slug of a tongue along his teeth, which looked yellow.

He was dead. He looked dead.

So how was he…

Beth.

One of them was on Beth. Mrs Potstello.

She was holding Beth and pressing her back against the window and—

And then Nisha ran.

She ran away from Harry.

She ran over to the window.

She grabbed the chair by the window and she lifted it and she smashed it and...

The window didn't smash open.

The chair just bounced back towards the floor.

Nisha stood there. Frozen. Mrs Potstello moving her open mouth towards Beth's neck. Beth crying. She could see her *screaming*. And Mrs Thompson and Mr Rawcliffe running towards her, too.

She stood there in the middle of the class, surrounded by dead kids, when she noticed something. Yuri, he was called. Little Yuri. Lying in the middle of the kids. And then he shot up. He must've been playing dead, like a dog. But he shot up, and he ran towards the door, and...

And Nisha wanted to tell him to stop. She wanted to tell him to stop because she saw Mr Rawcliffe and Mrs Thompson go running after him. And then she saw Ginger Harry get up, too, and then...

Mrs Potstello.

Which meant...

Nisha turned around and saw Beth standing at the window.

The window had a crack in it. And Beth's head was bleeding. She must've banged her head against it. But she was okay now. She was okay because Mrs Potstello was gone.

But...

Don't look, Beth signed.

Nisha felt sick. She saw the shadows in the corners of her eyes. And she saw Beth's wide, crying eyes staring out of the classroom, out towards their schoolmate Little Yuri, and whatever was happening to him.

Beth pushed the cracked glass until it stretched like spiderwebs and then smashed.

She climbed out the window. Waved at Nisha.

And then lifted her hands.

We go now.

Nisha stood there. Looked around the classroom at the blood. At the dead kids. And looked at the spot where Ginger Harry lay before. Dead. She was sure of it. But not dead.

She took a deep breath. Smelled metal in the air. Tasted salt on her lips.

And then she walked over towards that window, towards Beth, towards whatever was out there.

DWAYNE

* * *

Dwayne sat in the passenger seat of Nico's hire car, and he could only watch as Nico turned towards him and threw himself at him.

Nico landed on top of Dwayne. He grabbed the sides of his face. He dug his long fingernails into the sides of Dwayne's head, making it split with pain. The metallic tang of blood filled the confines of the car, mingling with the acrid stench of sweat.

Dwayne pushed back against Nico. For a man who'd just passed out right beside him, he had an awful lot of strength right now. Nico's teeth snapped together. His eyes protruded from his skull. His breath smelled awful, like bins left out in the summer sun.

And he was getting closer to Dwayne's neck.

Closer to *biting* him? Biting him just like he'd bitten Gary? And just like *he'd* been bitten?

"Nico," Dwayne gasped. "It's me, man. It's me."

But Nico didn't seem to hear. He just kept on pushing Dwayne back in his seat. Dwayne pushed him back with all his strength, stretching out his arms to hold him back.

But Nico kept on pushing.

Nico kept on pressing his bony arm against Dwayne's neck. Choking him. Making it hard to breathe. Impossible to breathe.

Dwayne's heart raced. His temples pulsated. His neck ached. He tried to gasp for air, tried to inhale, but he couldn't, he just couldn't.

He closed his burning eyes and he saw...

Mum.

Mum, in that nursing home.

The fear in her eyes.

"I just want to get out," she said. "I just want to get out."

He pushed back against Nico. Pushed back, as hard as he could.

And then he jolted forward.

An almighty crash exploded in the car.

The sound of glass smashing and metal crumbling surrounded him.

And that pressure. That pressure, holding him down. It'd gone. He was free.

He opened his eyes.

The cars in front looked different, somehow. He glanced up in the rear-view. The rear windshield was in pieces. There was a bus behind him. It's alarm ringing out, piercing. That bus wasn't there before. It must've slammed into Nico's car.

Shit. He hoped Nico had the cash to cover the costs. He could use his share of the...

Wait. No. What the hell was he even thinking?

Somehow, he had a feeling recouping the cost of a hire car was going to be the least of the rental place's concerns the way things were going.

But that windshield. That broken windshield. And the lack of pressure on his chest.

He had an opportunity.

He had a chance.

He had…

A gasp.

A grunt, from…

Wait. That wasn't from Nico.

It was.

A figure.

A figure, appearing at the passenger window.

Standing up. Rising, out of nowhere.

Gary.

Only… Gary didn't look like he looked before. There was none of the screaming after just having his arm gnawed on by a possessed Nico. And his arm looked in a pretty terrible state. Leaking a shitload of blood.

And…

His eyes.

His eyes were dead. Grey. He looked in Dwayne's vague direction. But he didn't look *at* Dwayne.

He looked… *through* Dwayne.

Dwayne looked back at him. Then at Nico, who scrambled from side to side on the dashboard.

He saw that same deadness to their eyes.

That same animalistic manner to their movements.

And he might not understand it, but he understood one thing.

He needed to get out of this car.

The front windscreen was out of bounds. Nico was too much of a hurdle.

And the passenger door. That was jammed. He'd tried it already.

He turned around and he saw the broken rear windshield.

Damn it. Here goes nothing…

He grabbed the backs of the seats.

And then he dragged himself into the back of the car.

Towards the windshield.

Something grabbed his ankle. Tightened its grip around it. A hand. Nico's hand. Gary's hand. He wasn't sure. But he needed to get it off him. He needed to kick it away.

He booted back. Flailed aimlessly. "Get off," he gasped. "Get the fuck…"

He felt his boot connect with something solid. A loud gasp echoed through the car.

And that hand. It loosened its grip.

Dwayne was free.

He didn't stop to think about it. He couldn't. Not anymore.

He just pulled himself towards that windshield.

Dragged himself through it.

He plunged through the broken window. The shards of glass sliced through his skin like daggers. The taste of blood filled his mouth as he dragged himself further, then tumbled onto the unforgiving concrete road, pain radiating right through his body.

He lay there a few seconds. And then…

Shit.

The bag.

The money bag.

He looked up. Turned around. Into the car.

Nico and Gary. Both in the car. Both trying to scramble their way past the back seats, and towards that broken windshield.

And the money bag, right there between them.

Dwayne stood there in the middle of the road. He saw the mass of traffic, all around him. He saw smoke in the distance, rising above. He heard screaming. Smelled burning. Tasted blood.

And as he stood there, wincing, his body on fire… as much as Dwayne wanted that cash, as much as Mum's disappointed, tearful eyes filled his mind, and as much as that plane to the Costa del Sol disintegrated, right before his very eyes… he knew he was leaving without the cash.

He looked at Nico. His glazed eyes. The blood on his mouth. His ghostly pale face.

And he shook his head.

No.

He wasn't giving up on the cash.

His cash was his reason for living, now.

He'd figure out a way.

He'd find a way to get it.

He'd...

A groan.

Right behind him.

He froze. The hairs on the back of his neck stood on end.

Had he heard a groan? Or was it in his head? Maybe it was in his head. 'Cause his ears were ringing, and his heart was racing, and he'd witnessed enough shit to scar him for life in the space of a few moments.

He turned around.

Slowly.

Three figures.

Three figures, standing there, between the cars.

Staring at him.

Or rather... staring *through* him.

Just like...

Just like Gary.

Just like Nico.

Just like...

Before Dwayne could even process his thoughts, the three figures raced down the road, right towards him.

PETE

* * *

Pete staggered down the road and he couldn't stop thinking about the girl's scream.

The summer sun beat down from above, burning his face. Cars surrounded him. Some of them were abandoned. Others, people sat inside, honking their horns, trying to part the mass of traffic in front of them. Occasionally, he heard a bang. A crash. The sound of yet another collision. This was pandemonium. This was chaos.

And it was getting worse.

But it was that scream he heard. That scream, replaying in his mind, again and again.

The look on the girl's face.

The tears in her eyes.

"Please," she begged, as she sat there in that car. "Please."

And then, almost by instinct, grabbing that car door and opening it and…

No. No, don't think about it. Best not to think about it. Because what else was he supposed to do in that situation? These people. These rage-fuelled bastards. They were about to kill him. They were about to rip him to shreds.

So what was he supposed to do?

How was he supposed to react?

It was survival. Pure survival instinct kicking in.

He'd done what anyone would do.

That was the truth of it. Because as much as he hated to admit it… he didn't know that kid. He didn't know who she was. So instinct drove him. Instinct just kicked in and it *made* him act the way he had.

That wasn't his decision. It wasn't his call. It was instinct. Pure instinct.

It wasn't his fault.

Right?

He walked further down the road. Smoke rose in the distance. Sirens surrounded him.

But as much as he tried to convince himself he'd done the only thing he could do… those agonised screams followed him.

A movement. A bang, to his right. He looked around. No one there. Nothing there. Or rather… someone. A woman. Blonde hair. Specks of blood in that hair. Staggering along. Limping. Bleeding from her Achilles. She needed an ambulance. She needed a hospital. She needed help.

And she wasn't the only one. Another bang to his left. Crying. Wailing. A man, in his twenties. Long hair. Heavy metal T-shirt. Holding a woman in his arms, by the side of his car.

"Mum," he whimpered. "Wake up. Please wake up. Please."

Pete turned away and walked further down the road. The horror welled up in his chest. He tasted stomach acid. Felt dizzy. Felt sick. He was gonna throw up. He was gonna vomit. 'Cause this. All this. This shit didn't happen over here. Maybe in some third-world country, but not here. This kind of suffering didn't happen in Britain.

He reached into his pocket. Pulled out his phone. Scrolled down his contacts to Helen and tried her again.

"I'm sorry, but the person you called is not available. Please try again l—"

"Fuck," Pete shouted.

He clutched his phone tight. The signal bar was empty. It shouldn't be empty. Not down here. What the hell was happening? What the hell was going on?

He stuffed his phone in his pocket. Looked at the surrounding cars. There was no way he was getting a vehicle off this road. He was gonna have to walk off this road. Hopefully find a bike along the way. And then he was gonna head back home to Helen.

'Cause that's what he needed to do. He really didn't have a choice.

He thought about Stan. He thought about Colin. And then he thought about the other ones. That group of rage-heads hurtling towards him. Chasing him.

And as much as he didn't want to believe it—as much as he wanted to believe it was bullshit—it looked like it was linked. It was all linked.

He shook his head. A knot tightened in his chest. A sickening punch in his stomach.

Helen.

Helen was the only one he could think of.

He looked at the cars. The way they filled this busy road. He looked at the smoke rising in the distance. He looked at the flames in the city centre. He listened to the sirens, and the screams, and he tasted the blood on his lips.

He knew what he *should* do. He knew exactly what he committed to when he put on the badge.

But there were some things that went beyond the badge.

Way, way beyond the badge.

He grabbed his police badge.

Looked at it. The sun bouncing against it in his hand.

He remembered the day he'd got it. The pride he'd felt. No one was bullying him again. No one was ever telling him what to do, ever again.

And then he took a deep breath of the muggy air.

Dropped it to the ground.

He looked up, away from the city centre, and over towards the trees, where he knew the suburbs were.

Where he knew his *home* was.

Family before duty.

He knew what he needed to do.

He took another deep breath, and then he walked.

DAVID

* * *

David saw Mrs Kirkham racing down the garden as fast as she could and he wondered when in the name of hell this nightmare was ever gonna end.

Barking. Behind him. That dog. That bitten dog, shaking, terrified. And Mrs Kirkham... okay, not exactly *racing* down the garden. 'Cause her right ankle was snapped, and kept on collapsing underneath her.

But for a woman whose right ankle was snapped—for a woman in her eighties whose right ankle was snapped—she was moving remarkably fast.

Mrs Kirkham gasped. Blood spluttered out of her mouth. Her red eyes cried bloody tears right down her face.

And behind, that dog kept on barking. Kept on yelping.

He turned around. The golden retriever. That bloody patch on its rear left side. Its tail tucked between its legs. Its hackles, right on end.

He couldn't get sentimental right now. He needed to get to the hospital. He needed to get to Keira. He needed to know his daughter was okay.

But this dog...

He couldn't just leave it here in his garden.

"Shit," he muttered. "What the hell am I doing?"

And then he ran towards the dog.

The dog's ears sunk further into its head. It barked at David. Snarled at him, then barked louder.

"It's okay, lad," David said. "We're gonna get you out of here, okay? We're gonna get you out of here."

A gasp echoed behind him. Closer behind him than he wanted to admit. Shit. Mrs Kirkham. She was close. She was close, and she sounded... possessed.

He ran further down the garden. The dog glared at him. Backed up. His hackles rose further. He barked.

"Come on, boy," David said. "Don't make this difficult for me."

He reached out to grab the dog.

The dog snapped.

Snapped at his hand.

David yanked his hand back. "Shit. Come on, lad. Hardly a way to make friends, is it?"

And then he heard that cry behind him again.

He didn't want to look back. Didn't want to accept that Mrs Kirkham was anywhere near him.

But at the same time, he knew he didn't have a choice.

He turned around.

Mrs Kirkham was just metres away from him.

She ran down the garden with more ease now. Quicker. Shit. That wasn't good news.

But there was still a window of opportunity.

There was still enough time.

David turned back round to the dog.

He saw his collar. Rufus. Rufus? What kind of a name was that for a human, let alone a dog?

"Rufus," David said. "We're gonna have to get along here,

okay? Because if we can't get along... I have a bad feeling that lady back there ain't gonna be so nice to you."

Rufus barked at David. His back legs shook. Urine trickled out of him, its acrid stench filling David's nostrils.

David inched further towards Rufus. Even though Mrs Kirkham was getting closer, he focused all his attention on Rufus. On forming that connection with Rufus. On making that bond with him.

"You're gonna have to trust me, lad," David said. Inching closer towards him. Outstretching his hand. "We're gonna have to get along. Or..."

And then he touched Rufus's head.

He stroked him. Ruffled his fur. And Rufus's growling eased. His rapid panting slowed. And his hackles lowered. Just a little.

"That's it," David said. "We're gonna be okay. We're gonna get out of here. We're—"

And then David felt the pressure on his back.

He felt those hands, gripping his shoulders.

And then he felt something digging into his skin; something...

He collapsed to the ground. Gasping in his right ear. A sour stench filling his nostrils. Mrs Kirkham. She was on him. She'd caught him. She'd...

He turned over.

Mrs Kirkham glared down at him with angry eyes. She snapped her bloody teeth. Those teeth didn't look even. They looked...

Wait.

False.

False teeth.

David reached up.

He grabbed Ms Kirkham's top teeth.

And then he yanked them out of her mouth, and tossed them aside.

Mrs Kirkham kept on biting. Her bottom set of false teeth

sunk into her gums. Blood and pus oozed out, and spilled all over David's face.

He pushed her back. Grabbed the bottom set of falsies, tried to yank them away, but they wouldn't loosen. Shit. What was he doing?

He held on to those teeth. He pulled with as much force as he could. And then...

Something crumbled between his fingers.

Mrs Kirkham's false teeth. The entire bottom set was falling apart in his hand. Teeth rained down on him, covering him. Teeth, and blood, and pus, and God knows what else.

He pushed her back as she tried to gum at him. She tumbled back, then slammed against the grass in a twitching, gasping heap. His hands. His hands were covered in blood. He could feel little lumps of tooth clinging to his face. Shit. He was gonna puke. He was...

Rufus.

He turned around.

Rufus wasn't barking anymore.

He wasn't growling.

He was just standing there.

Staring.

"Rufus," David said.

His hackles weren't up. Progress. And his tail, it wasn't tucked between his legs anymore. Wow. Graeme fucking Hall over here. The dog whisperer himself.

"Good lad," David said. "We're gonna get you out of here. You're gonna be okay. We're both gonna be..."

And then Rufus turned to him.

He looked right at him. Right at him, with these glazed eyes.

Tilted his head.

Wait. Something wasn't right.

"Rufus?" David said.

Rufus tilted his head again.

His glass-like eyes peered at David, just like...

"Mrs Kirkham," he said.

He saw the bloody mark on Rufus's back.

Fuck.

What if—

And then Rufus growled.

He snarled, his long, sharp teeth glistening in the summer sun.

And then he threw himself at David.

KEIRA

* * *

Keira saw Omar and Gavin racing down the corridor towards her, and she knew she needed to get out of here.

She turned around. Ran. Sprinted as fast as she could. She needed to get away. She needed to get to those double doors, right ahead of her. She needed to get through those doors, and then she needed to get outside, and she needed to get far, far away from here.

A screech echoed down the corridor, from the mortuary. Keira turned. It was the woman. The one she'd seen moments earlier. She wasn't standing still anymore. She was running towards Keira, too.

Fuck.

She raced further down the corridor. One step at a time. Screams bounced against the walls of these narrow, tomblike corridors. The amber lights flickered above. Alarms rang out. Keira heard distant screaming. She was trapped down here. She was trapped down here and they were going to catch her and—

No.

Be strong.

Keep it together. Like you always have.

Those double doors edged closer. But it felt like she was running in slow motion. Like she was in a nightmare. In a bad dream.

She ran further towards those doors. Just get through those, and then get down the stairs, and then...

Pressure.

Pressure on her left ankle.

Oh shit.

Oh shit oh shit oh—

She hurtled forward. Slammed her face against the hard tiled floor. Her nose exploded with agony. The hot metal of blood filled her mouth. And that pressure on her ankle. A hand. It was a hand. She needed to get away. She needed to get it off her. She needed to get away.

The hand tightened around her ankle.

Shit. It was getting tighter.

She looked over her shoulder.

Her stomach sank.

All three of them. Omar. Blood still oozing out of his neck—but also out of his mouth now, too. Gavin, whose guts dangled in front of him, trailing on the stained white floor behind him.

And the woman from down the corridor. She was here too.

All of them reached down for Keira.

All of their teeth snapped together.

All of their faces got closer, closer...

Keira couldn't breathe. She squeezed her eyes shut. She thought of Mum. Mum, holding her hand. Walking along a beach. Water crashing against the sand. The sound of laughter—her own laughter. The sickly-sweet taste of vanilla ice cream on her lips. And...

Dad.

Standing there in the distance.

Smile on his face.

Waving.

A knot tightened in Keira's chest. Tears filled her eyes.

"I'm sorry," she whimpered. "I'm sorry. I'm—"

"Get off her!"

A large clang echoed above.

What the hell was that?

And where the hell was that voice coming from?

"Get up, Keira. Get up and run!"

What the hell?

Keira opened her eyes.

Gavin was still on top of her. But Omar and the other woman, their attention was elsewhere.

Their attention was...

"Jean?" Keira said.

Jean was holding a fire extinguisher. She was swinging it around in the air. Spraying it at Omar, and at the other woman. Drawing their attention away from Keira.

Jean looked down at Keira. Right into her eyes. Jean was covered in tears and blood.

"Get away, Keira," she shouted. "Run. Run. Now!"

Keira shook her head. "I can't—I can't leave—"

"You're a young woman with so much more to live for, my girl."

"But you're—"

"The cancer. It's back. And it's not good this time. It's over, sis. It's over."

A crushing weight crashed down on Keira's shoulders. The cancer. Jean's cancer. It was supposed to have gone into remission. She was supposed to be okay.

"Just promise me one thing," Jean shouted, as Gavin turned his attention towards her too. As all three of them descended on Jean, as she drew them further and further away from Keira.

No. This couldn't be real. This couldn't be happening.

"You get up," Jean shouted, staggering further back. "You get up and you find Omar's daughter. She doesn't have anyone else. She'll be at school. She's—"

And then, out of nowhere, another man lunged through the door from the wards.

He grabbed Jean's throat. And then he sunk his teeth into her. Ripped out her throat. Blood gushed out, everywhere, painting the walls red.

Keira screamed. Covered her mouth, instinctively, as she watched Omar, Gavin and the woman—presumably Hailee—descend upon her. As she watched them grab her. As she watched them rip at her face, and bite her neck and her arms, and more and more blood puddle out.

Keira held her hand over her mouth. Her heart raced. She tried to breathe. But she couldn't. Her throat. Her chest. Everything. It was all frozen. It was all solid. It was all…

Jean looked at her, as the mob ripped her to pieces.

She looked right into her eyes, as her blood splattered up over the walls, and the lights, and everywhere.

As Omar tore into her right shoulder; as he yanked the skin and the flesh away, exposing the bone.

"Go," Jean gargled. "Omar's… daughter. Go…"

Keira shook her head. Tears clouded her vision. She didn't want to get up. She didn't want to run. She didn't want to leave Jean behind.

"Go…" Jean said.

And then she started screaming.

Keira covered her ears with her shaking hands. She tried to stand, but she couldn't; her legs were like jelly, and every muscle felt like stone.

Go. Omar's daughter. Go…

"I'm sorry, Jean," she gasped. "I'm sorry."

She stood up. Turned around. Tried to run towards those

double doors. Behind her, she heard the sound of flesh being torn. Of blood being gargled, like Dad used to gargle mouthwash over the sink in the morning.

And she heard those agonised, pained whimpers.

"Omar…" she cried. "Omar's… Omar's…"

Keira cried. "I'm sorry," she said. "I'm sorry. I'm…"

And then she collapsed into the double doors.

Tumbled through them.

Slammed them shut.

Grabbed a mop from a bucket by her side, and wedged it through the handles.

She backed up. Heart racing. Ears ringing. Shaking. Crying.

Behind those doors, she could still hear Jean, screaming.

"It's okay," she muttered. "It's okay. It's…"

Footsteps.

Right behind her.

Her stomach sank.

She wasn't alone.

NISHA

* * *

Nisha walked away from the school with Beth and she felt worried sick.

It was warm. Nisha's skin burned hot. Sweat poured down her face, all salty on her lips. She could taste that nasty tang of suncream too. Dad always made sure she wore suncream in the summer, even when it wasn't sunny. Grandma died of skin cancer, and it made him afraid of the sun. Nisha didn't really understand how anyone could be afraid of the sun. It was just a big warm ball of light. She didn't know how the sun could give anyone cancer.

The car park ahead was empty and quiet. There were a few cars lined up on the right, where the teachers parked. But the other spaces—the spaces where parents came to pick them up—were empty. And that made Nisha feel even more weird. Because she thought when she got out the school that Dad would be waiting here in the car park for her. That he'd heard about the horrible things in the school and he'd come to save her, and Beth's mum and dad had come to save her too, and that so many other kids had got out the school, got away, and everything was okay.

But no one was here.

The air smelled of burning, like whenever Dad tried to cook anything more advanced than pasta. She could taste metal on her lips. Blood. Her heart pounded against her chest.

The bodies.

The bodies of the other schoolkids. Lying there in a bloody heap.

Ginger Harry, rising from the floor. Trying to bite her. Trying to...

She couldn't breathe. Her chest, it was all tight. It felt like she had a snake around her neck, getting tighter, tighter, and the air was hot and she was dizzy and colours filled her vision and—

A hand.

A hand on her shoulder.

She spun around.

Beth stared at her with wide eyes. Her face was pale. Little beads of sweat trickled down her cheeks. She was shaking. She looked... sicker. Sicker than when Nisha first saw her. But then Nisha probably looked sicker, too. The shock. That made people look sick. Dad told her that when Mum went away. That's why he looked so tired all the time, and why he couldn't do the things he used to enjoy without feeling like he'd run a marathon. The shock. And his "black dog", as he called it, even though Nisha didn't know why he called it that because every black dog she'd met was nice and friendly. It was the yellow ones she was scared of.

Blood trickled from Beth's left arm. She kept on hiding it. Kept on moving it away whenever Nisha tried to look at it. She must've caught it on the broken window when they'd climbed out. That's what she had to believe. That's what she had to tell herself.

Beth raised her hands, making sure that bloody mark was covered. *Where now?*

A knot tightened in Nisha's chest. She looked around the car park, then back at Beth. *Wait for parents?*

No. Can't wait. No parents.

It was hard to understand what Beth was saying. Hard to understand what she was signing. She wasn't great at signing. But she was better than most people, and better than any other kid Nisha had ever met, so that was something.

Nisha swallowed a lump in her throat. She didn't want to go anywhere. If she went anywhere, Dad might get here for her, and if she wasn't here, then what then? He'd be scared. He'd be afraid. He would do anything to find her; he'd do anything for Nisha. And if she just walked away? No. She couldn't do that.

Bad people. School. Noises. Screams.

Nisha saw Beth signing and then she saw the look in her wide eyes. The way she peered over at the school. The noises. She could hear things coming from the school.

Noises.

Screams.

There were very few moments in Nisha's life where she actually felt kind of happy that she couldn't hear. Not being able to hear was rubbish. Not being able to hear made her weak. So weak.

But right now... she was glad she couldn't hear.

Scared about walking away. Parents come soon.

Beth squinted. Then she shrugged. She wasn't understanding Nisha. Shit.

Nisha closed her eyes. Took a deep breath. Then she tried to form some other, easier-to-sign words.

Wait for parents.

She opened her eyes. Beth nodded. Like she understood. Which for a moment, made Nisha feel relieved.

But then Beth raised her shaking hands. Started signing. And it was all gibberish at first. It was all just... well, *noise*.

And then, piece by piece, as Nisha squinted, as she tried to understand... she started to get it. She started to understand.

Not sure anyone coming.

Those words. They were like a punch to Nisha's chest.

Because that couldn't be true. Dad always came. Parents always came to help, didn't they?

But then she thought of the bodies lying in the Year Two classroom. The blood on the walls. Mrs Thompson, Mr Rawford and Mrs Potstello chasing them all; tearing them all up…

This wasn't a normal day.

She saw something, then. Noticed something, in the corner of her eye. Up the path, on the road. A man. A man on the ground. His eyes were wide. His mouth was even wider. He was—he looked like he was screaming.

And there was someone on top of him.

A lady.

Holding him down.

Biting his neck.

Ripping his skin and his muscle away and making blood pool out of him.

Nisha felt cold inside. She felt sick. The teachers. The teachers in the school. And now on the road, it looked like there'd been a car accident, and it looked like…

It looked like whatever was happening at school was happening *outside* school, too.

Beth touched Nisha's arm again, making her jump.

Not safe here.

And as much as Nisha didn't want to admit it… she was beginning to feel like Beth was right.

She caught a glimpse of that bloody mark on Beth's arm, as she turned around, and started to walk away, towards the back of the school.

And this time, when she saw the blood, she was pretty sure she saw something else that made the butterflies fly around her stomach again.

Tooth marks.

DWAYNE

* * *

Dwayne stared at the rucksack of cash sitting inside Nico's car, and he didn't have a clue what he was going to do.

Nico and Gary dragged themselves to the smashed rear windshield of the car Dwayne had just escaped from. Dwayne's body was on fire. Pain. Splitting pain in his arms, right down his back and his legs. He'd cut himself on the broken glass. And cut himself pretty bad from the feel of things. He felt exhausted. He felt broken. He felt weak.

But he was still here.

He was still alive.

And he still had an opportunity.

The rucksack of cash stared back at him, between Gary and Nico. Gary growled, and gnawed at the driver's seat. Nico looked completely *gone*. Bloodshot eyes bulged out of his face. Blood trickled out of his ears. Blood. Blood, everywhere.

And it didn't make sense. None of it made sense. Nico. He'd been bitten. Bitten by someone back at the car park, where he'd got this car. And then he'd taken a turn for the worse. And then he'd bitten Gary. And now *Gary* was acting like a maniac, too.

He didn't understand it. He didn't understand it one bit.

But right now, as crazy as it sounded... he could see a link. One sole, mental link.

The bites.

The guy who'd bitten Nico. Nico. And now Gary.

And now the pair of them were trying to bite him.

And besides, just to make it worse, there were three more of these nutters, racing down the street, right towards him.

Dwayne looked at the bag of cash. He looked over his shoulder, at those approaching lunatics. He looked back at the cash again. He thought about Spain. He thought about how this was supposed to be the start of something new for him. It was supposed to be the start of a new life. A better life. A cleaner life, away from all his "contacts", and all his debts, and all the crime.

But more than anything... it was Mum he thought of.

The care home. The publicly funded care home. Worst of the worst. Because he couldn't afford anything better. He couldn't afford to pay for proper care. And he couldn't afford to move her into private accommodation with a carer, the ideal scenario.

Dwayne had done some bad shit. He wasn't an idiot. He was no stranger to crime. He'd stolen from people. Good people, no doubt. And... he'd hurt people, too. He didn't want to think about the worst hurt he'd caused. He preferred not thinking about that.

He pushed that to the back of his mind.

The Bristol job.

A shiver crept down his spine.

Yeah. He'd rather not think about the Bristol job.

He'd done some bad things. But he had his reasons.

And right now, he realised he didn't have a choice about what he was going to do.

He had to get away from here.

He had to run.

He had to…

A shout.

Someone running down the road beside him.

Screaming.

And in the car, he saw them turn.

Gary and Nico. Both of them turned their attention from Dwayne. Both of them looked at the screaming man, running down the street.

And that momentary turn of attention. That momentary shift. It sparked something in Dwayne's mind.

An idea.

A horrible idea.

An idea that made a weight build in his chest, just as heavy as the one when he was down in Bristol.

A choice he had.

A decision he had to make.

That man. That man sprinting down the road. Bleeding from his left ankle.

And…

Gary and Nico.

And the rucksack of money.

Dwayne looked at that sprinting man. He looked at the three figures, who'd turned their attention towards him, too. And then he looked back at the car.

And he didn't even allow himself a moment to think.

He rushed over to the door.

Grabbed it.

Looked at Nico and Gary inside there. Snapping their teeth together. Gnawing at the glass.

And then he saw *his* face, in the reflection.

Saw the guilt in his eyes.

He swallowed a lump in his throat.

Was he doing this?

Was he really doing this?

And then he thought of Mum.

He grabbed the handle, opened the car door, and both Nico and Gary scrambled out of it.

Gary ran off towards the screaming man. He was faster than him. And he was joined by three others. The three who were chasing Dwayne before.

He saw them tackle the man to the ground. Saw them push him down. He heard the man cry out, heard him squeal like a pig. And then he saw blood. So much blood.

His vision clouded. The world started to spin around him.

Brighton.

"Please. No. Please!"

And then...

He closed his eyes. Swallowed a lump in his throat.

He'd done it for Mum. He'd done it like he'd done so many things before. So many bad things before.

This was the final bad thing. The final bad thing he was ever going to have to do. And soon everything was going to be okay. Soon, he wouldn't have to do any bad things again.

And then he grabbed the rucksack of cash, and dragged it out of the car.

When he turned around, he saw someone standing opposite him.

Staring right at him with those empty eyes.

His stomach sank.

Shit.

Oh shit.

Nico was standing right in front of him.

He hadn't joined the crowd.

And judging by the look in his eyes... he wasn't ready to let him leave without his share of the cash.

PETE

* * *

Pete ran down the motorway and tried not to look back over his shoulder—even though he kind of had to, to stay alive.

It was boiling. His damp shirt chafed at his armpits. The air hung with the stench of sweat. Probably mostly his own sweat. It was sunny, but the sky overhead cast a grey pallor. Gusts of wind stirred up swirling debris. Broken glass crunched under Pete's boots with every cautious step, a constant reminder of this weird, shattered world he suddenly found himself in.

He was a fair way away from his police car now. He had no idea how long he'd been running. A sense of foreboding settled deep in Pete's gut as he glimpsed one unsettling scene after another unfolding on each side of the motorway. Figures, distorted and frenzied, clashed with each other in violent confrontations. What he initially dismissed as random acts of aggression were beginning to make way for a horrifying truth: this whole damned city was tearing itself apart, right before his damned eyes.

Blood stained the road, its vibrant crimson contrasting starkly with the grey tarmac. A metallic tang hung in the air, intermingling with the scent of burning rubber and a faint undertone of sweat, urine, faeces. The once orderly lanes of the motorway now resembled chaotic battlegrounds, strewn with empty cars. Some of those cars had people trapped inside them, angrily trying to break free. Other bodies lay on the road, in the sun, carrying the kinds of wounds Pete hadn't seen in all his years as a cop. And even though his heart clenched with every glimpse of brutality... he knew he needed to keep his distance. He knew he needed to ignore his instincts. His instincts to get involved. To fulfil his duties as a police officer.

He had to survive.

For Helen.

But he couldn't shake what he was witnessing from the forefront of his consciousness. Down on the street below the motorway, a group of individuals, driven to madness, tore into each other with unbridled ferocity. Their eyes glazed over, devoid of reason, consumed by an insatiable hunger—a hunger Pete couldn't understand.

And amongst the chaos, Pete caught fleeting glimpses of so many harrowing scenes. A mother, bleeding from her back, huddled protectively over her son, whispering to him as tears rolled down her face. "It'll be okay, Tommy. It'll be okay." But it was pretty clear that Tommy was dead.

Further in the distance, a black man, eyes wide with terror, desperately tried to break free from the merciless grasp of a paramedic.

A cacophony of guttural growls and anguished screams echoed in his ears, a haunting symphony of this city's demise.

Pete kept running. A mixture of fear and determination propelled him forward. He scanned the horizon, searching for an escape, an exit from this nightmare. Every passing moment intensified the realisation of the situation: a situation far more sinister than just random acts of violence.

As Pete pressed on, the motorway stretching endlessly before him, he felt the weight of the world closing in. He saw so many people, suffering. He saw so much fear. He saw so much pain. He saw so many people in need.

Then he remembered what happened on the road.

Opening that door.

Opening the car door so those wankers could get to the little girl.

Using her as a distraction, so he could get away.

A bitter taste filled his mouth. A wave of sickness crashed over him.

No. He couldn't think about that.

He just had to keep going.

He just had to keep moving.

He saw the motorway bridge up ahead. He had an idea. He needed to get off this bridge. But he couldn't take one of the junctions. The junctions were a nightmare. He'd seen a couple already, and the scene was the same at every one: so many cars, so many people, so much panic, and so much fear.

But if he could get to the next motorway bridge, he could find a way down from it. He could find a way down, and then he could climb down to the street and make his way back home; back to Helen.

He gritted his teeth and tried to keep his shit together even though he was very much falling apart inside. His teeth chattered against one another. "You've got this, Pete," he muttered, as tears rolled down his cheeks, as a surge of guilt and of pure panic shot right through his chest. "You've got this. And you're going to be okay."

He grabbed his phone again with his shaking hand. Hit Helen's number. Fully expected it to cut out again.

But…

But this time, it started ringing.

"Shit," Pete said. He didn't even know what he was gonna say. He didn't expect her to answer. He thought it was just going to cut out again.

It rang, until eventually, someone answered.

"Helen?"

No noise. Just static.

Breathing.

Like someone was there, on the other end.

Listening.

"Helen," Pete said. "There's something happening. If you don't know already, there's something happening. Something bad. I'm heading down the motorway. I should be at our's soon. But..."

A cough.

A *bloke's* cough.

And then the line went dead.

Pete stood there. Yeah, *stood* there. Stopped running, clearly. He looked down at the phone in his shaking hand. That bloke. Who the hell was that? And where the hell was Helen?

His face burned. She was with another man. Or someone had attacked her. Someone had attacked her and she was in danger. She needed help. She needed help.

He shook his head. Didn't want to get too lost or too absorbed in his thoughts right now. He was already lost in them enough as it was.

He ran to the motorway bridge. Stopped when he reached it. Looked across it. The road down there looked quieter. One silver Nissan had crashed into a red Mercedes. A kid's bike lay on its side. But that was about the limit of the damage down there, as far as he could tell—even if he knew damn well that behind the closed doors of those perfect-looking suburban houses, there would be many secrets waiting for him.

Secrets he didn't want to find.

He took a deep breath. Swallowed a lump in his throat.

He had to get off this bridge somehow. He had to get off here, and then he had to get down the road and he had to get back home.

Because Helen was in danger.

Helen needed him.

He went to take a step closer to the bridge when he heard something right behind him.

Something that sent a shiver right down his spine, once again.

A growl.

Scrambling.

And then... a voice.

"Help. Help. Please."

DAVID

* * *

David saw the dog fly towards him and right away he knew he was in deep shit.

David stumbled backwards, his heart pounding in his chest as he desperately tried to evade the frenzied dog's snapping jaws. Fear gripped him, the primal instinct for survival surging through his veins. His mind raced, struggling to make sense of the chaos unfolding before him.

The golden retriever—Rufus—barked at him. He lifted his paws out at David. He opened his mouth. And David could only brace himself, as he stood there at the bottom of his garden. Brace himself for the dog to land on him. Brace himself for the dog's teeth to sink into his skin, to rip his throat out.

But...

Rufus didn't bite him.

He licked him.

And then he dropped to the ground. Cowered behind David.

Whining.

David stared down at Rufus. Rufus's eyes were wild with fear and distress, mirroring David's own confusion, no doubt. Its snarls were mixed with desperate whimpers, as if torn between its natural instinct to protect, and an unseen terror that its own existence was threatened. In a split second, the dog's entire demeanour seemed to have shifted, and instead of attacking, it cowered even further behind David, clearly seeking refuge and solace.

As Rufus nuzzled against his leg, David's initial fear gave way to a mixture of relief and curiosity. The dog, though frightened and wounded, posed no immediate threat after all. He was trembling. And he was looking for support.

"That's it," David said. Finally mustering up the courage to reach down and pat Rufus. He brushed his fingers against the dog's matted fur. The touch sparked a warmth inside David. His own shaking fingers eased. And momentarily, Rufus's shakes eased, too. David felt a connection forming between them. A sense of duty, opening up right before him. Rufus's tail thumped against the ground, out from underneath his legs. A flicker of trust sparked in its eyes.

But then David heard the gasp.

He turned around.

Mrs Kirkham raced back to her feet, towards David. Her bloodshot eyes bore into his soul. Her outstretched arms reached for him with an insatiable hunger. Fear surged through him once again. He might've dealt with her dentures. But this woman was still coming.

"Come on, Rufus," David said. "Only one way out of here."

He reached down. Picked Rufus up, still a little cautious of the dog, like Jim off Friday Night Dinner. He ran over to the fence on the right. Lowered Rufus over it. "That's it. You jump down there. I'll be right over."

He climbed up on top of the fence panel.

Looked back at Mrs Kirkham.

Blood trickled from her lips. She snarled. Gasped. Cried out.

And the way she cried, David almost felt sorry for her. He almost *sympathised* with her. Because as much as he didn't know what the hell was going on, Mrs Kirkham was a nice woman. A sweet woman.

And something had happened to make her this way.

He went to climb over the fence and drop down next door when he heard a crack beneath him.

He felt the fence start to wobble under his weight.

"Oh, shit..."

And then the fence gave way.

He slammed down against the ground. Face first in the freshly mowed grass next door. He staggered to his feet, eager not to let Mrs Kirkham anywhere near him again.

When he looked around, he saw...

The fence. The fence had crumbled in the middle. But Mrs Kirkham was wedged between a gap in it. Trying to break her way through. Stretching out her arms, trying to drag herself inside, but failing.

David felt a nudge on his right leg. He looked down. Saw Rufus beside him. Rufus panted. Looked over at the house—at Mrs Kirkham's place.

David looked up.

Up, at those ajar patio doors, and the darkness beyond.

And the bloody handprint, right in the middle of the window.

"Don't worry, lad," David said. "We're gonna get you out of here."

He swallowed a lump in his throat.

Looked back at Mrs Kirkham.

"I'll get you the help you need. One way or another. I promise."

And then he turned back around, and walked towards her back door.

In the darkness ahead, he swore he saw movement...

KEIRA

* * *

Keira heard the movement right behind her and her stomach sank to new depths.

She stood at the door to the corridor leading to the mortuary. She'd wedged a cleaner's mop through the door handles. Not the strongest material, but it was better than nothing. She could hear gasping, groaning in the corridor. The sound of damp flesh being torn away. Jean. Her best friend. Sacrificing herself for her. Giving up her life for her.

She closed her burning eyes. She heard that heavy breathing behind her. She didn't want to turn round. She couldn't face any more horror. This was a nightmare. This was a nightmare, and it had to end. This was a bad dream, and any minute now, she was going to wake up back at home—or even in her car out front of the hospital—and everything was going to be okay. She'd come to work. Tell Jean about the awful dream she'd had.

And maybe she'd even check on Dad.

A knot tightened in her stomach. Dad. She didn't think much about Dad these days. She tried not to, anyway.

But right now, frozen in this corridor, she found herself wanting to hear his voice. She found herself *wanting* him to comfort her.

And then she pushed those thoughts aside. She couldn't think like that. She couldn't start thinking about Dad now. Dad wasn't here. Dad was *never* going to be here. She didn't want to think about the last time she spoke to him. She didn't want to think about the last time she saw him.

She just wanted this nightmare to end.

That shuffling, right behind her. That shaky breathing.

Didn't matter how much she wanted this nightmare to end right now. She was going to have to turn around. She was going to have to compose herself. That's what Mum always taught her. She taught her to be strong. She taught her to stand up for herself. To fight for herself, and for what she believed was right.

She took as deep a breath as her tight muscles would allow, and she turned around.

Over by the lifts, under the flickering halogen lights, there was a man. He was sitting between the lifts. His head rested in his hands. He was wearing a blue surgeon's uniform. And he was muttering inaudible words under his breath.

Keira stood there. Still. Very still. Was this guy like Omar? Was he, for want of a better word, *infected* too?

"Please," the man muttered. "Please just—please just make this end. Please just make this end."

And then, suddenly, it dawned on Keira. She recognised this surgeon.

"Nitesh?"

Nitesh lifted his head. He looked over at Keira, terror glowing in his wide eyes.

"Are you—are you—"

"It's okay," Keira said. Trying to stay as calm as possible. Trying to fool herself that she was calm, for starters. "I'm okay. It's okay."

"Are you like the others?"

"No," Keira said, shaking her head. She held up her arms, mostly so Nitesh could see she hadn't been bitten—because it seemed like the rage spread through the bites, somehow. But holding up her arms probably wasn't the best idea, since she was covered in blood.

Nitesh buried his head in his hands again. He cried. Shook his head. Beneath him, Keira saw a puddle of orange fluid, and the strong scent of piss filled her nostrils.

"It's okay," she said, as she approached. "I haven't been bitten. I got away. Before they could get to me."

Nitesh shook his head. Whimpered into his hands.

Keira stood right in front of him. She crouched down. And then she put a hand on his shoulder.

Nitesh flinched. He looked up at her. Such terror in those wide eyes.

"You can trust me," Keira said. "We need to trust each other now. Right?"

Nitesh looked at Keira's hand. Then back at her arm, and her body, and her face. He looked like a child awakening from a bad dream. In a way, that's exactly what he was. Awakening from a dream he was certain was going to end terribly, only to find there was a spark of hope left in the world, after all.

"We need to get out of here," Keira said. "Okay? The hospital. It isn't safe."

"But there's so many patients here. So many friends."

A pain, right in the middle of Keira's chest. She wanted to help people. She wanted to help her friends. And she wanted to help as many patients as she could.

And then she remembered Jean. Jean's dying words to her.

Go. Omar's daughter. Go...

"I know—"

"I'm supposed to help people," Nitesh said. "I'm supposed to save people's lives. But I..."

Keira swallowed a bitter lump in her throat. "I know, Nitesh. I know. I'm a nurse. I'm supposed to care for people. I'm supposed to look after my patients. And my fellow nurses. We're supposed to have a bond. We're supposed to be united. Together. And walking away just feels so wrong. Walking away just makes me feel so, so sick inside..."

She thought of Jean. Gavin. Omar. Of all the screaming patients in the ward.

"But whatever we do, staying here and freezing won't help. So we need to get up. We need to walk down that staircase. And we need to get out of here."

Nitesh looked right into her eyes. He opened his mouth. And then he nodded. Went to say something—

A bang.

A bang at the double doors behind. Blocked only by a mop.

And behind that bang... snarls.

Gasps.

Shit.

They were here.

Keira turned around to Nitesh. She held both his hands. "You need to get up," she said.

Nitesh's breathing grew even more shallow. His eyes widened. His face went pale. Hyperventilating. An anxiety attack. Hyperventilating.

Another bang rattled the door behind.

Keira grabbed Nitesh's arms even tighter.

"Listen to me. You can get through this. We'll both get through this. But you need to get up. Both of us need to get out of this. Together. Right now. Okay?"

Nitesh looked into her eyes.

He opened his mouth.

"Yes—"

Another bang behind.

A louder gasp.

Keira turned around.

A hand. A hand and an arm smacked against the door. Trying to push it open. Trying to pull the mop away.

"Shit."

She dragged Nitesh to his shaking feet. Held his hand. And then she ran across the corridor, towards the door to the staircase.

"One step at a time, okay?" Keira said, pushing open the door. "One step at a..."

When the staircase door creaked open, she saw three figures standing there at the bottom of the first stretch of stairs.

They all turned around.

All looked at her.

All covered in blood.

"Shit," Keira said.

The three of them gasped, grunted, and ran as fast as they could at Keira.

"Fuck!"

Keira dragged Nitesh out of the staircase doors. The doors back to the wards rattled. More arms stuck through that gap between the doors. The mop. The mop was bending. It was going to snap. They didn't have much time.

"The lift," Keira said. "That's all we've got."

"But—"

The mop snapped.

The doors tumbled open.

"Now!" Keira shouted.

She dragged Nitesh towards the open lift door.

She threw herself inside. Slammed the "close" button.

And as she stood there, back to the very rear of the lift, she watched as they raced towards her.

Six. Seven. God, *loads* of them. They must've come from the wards. They didn't look like nurses, or surgeons. They looked like patients. Patients. The people she was supposed to be caring for. The people she was supposed to be protecting.

She pushed back against the wall as the lift doors crept shut.

As those snarling, screaming figures lurched closer towards them.

She held on to Nitesh's hand, as he cried, as he screamed.

"Please! Please God no!"

She watched as the door rattled.

As, for one moment, it froze.

As the infected at the front of the crowd outstretched its hand towards that door.

And then she watched as the door slammed shut.

She stood there. Listened to the banging at the other side of the lift door. Listened to the screaming. The shouting. Listened to it all, heart racing, a little piss trickling warm down the sides of her thighs, as Nitesh whimpered beside her, as she held on to him and told him to sshhh, told him everything was going to be okay.

She had no idea how long she stood there with Nitesh by her side, when she finally regained the ability to move.

She reached over to the lift numbers. Pressed the GF button, to take them right to the bottom.

Nothing happened.

She pressed it again. Not now. Not frigging now...

"That's what I was trying to tell you," Nitesh said.

"What?"

"The lift," he said. "It's out of order. The door locks. But it doesn't open."

Keira's stomach sank to... yes, even newer depths.

"What?" she said.

Nitesh looked up at her with wide, terrified eyes.

"We're trapped," he said. "We're trapped."

NISHA

* * *

Nisha held Beth's hand as she walked down the street and tried to imagine it was Dad right beside her.

It wasn't sunny anymore. It was cloudy. It was raining a bit. She liked the smell of rain on a warm day. It reminded her of when Dad took her to the campsite on holiday. He didn't have a lot of money like other mums and dads, and when he said they were going on holiday, Nisha thought he meant on an airplane. But instead they just got on the bus and went up to somewhere called Far Arnside, which didn't sound very exotic compared to some of the places her school friends went.

They stayed in a caravan for a weekend. It was nice. The weather was really bad. And the beach wasn't like beaches she saw on postcards, with blue water and golden sand and loads of sunbeds pushed up against each other. The beach was grey. There was no sand—there were big stones instead. And the sun never came out. It just rained all the time.

Dad was sad about it. He just wanted Nisha to have a nice holiday like the other kids. But Nisha did. She really did. She loved walking in the rain with Dad. She loved exploring the woods with him. And she loved watching him carve their initials onto that tree, and then being caught by some man who said he was going to report them to the police, and then running away with him, laughing.

She held Beth's hand and she really hoped she saw Dad again soon.

The road was long and scary. It didn't used to feel scary. Not with Dad. She knew where she had to go to get home now. Down this long road, then around the pond where the bigger kids played. And then she just had to go past the park, and the swings, and then she had to cross the busy road Dad never liked her crossing on her own, and then she was back home. It never felt like a long walk when she was with Dad. But today, it felt longer than ever.

There were loads of cars on the road. But they didn't have people in them. Some of them still had their doors open. Like people had just got out of the cars and run away.

There was blood on the road. And as far as Nisha could see, there was no one about. But it was quiet down this road. There weren't many houses down this road. As they got further down the road, maybe someone would be able to help them.

She looked around at Beth and her stomach sank.

Beth looked even paler than before. She wasn't walking easy. She kept wobbling from one foot to another. Her eyes kept closing, then suddenly opening again, like she was falling asleep and then waking up.

She didn't look well. And that mark on her arm. Where the blood was. Nisha kept worrying. She kept thinking about the kids back at school. The kids she'd seen lying there on the classroom floor. The ones she tried not to think about. Because thinking about them made her feel shaky, and made her feel scared.

Maybe Beth was the same. Maybe Beth was just like them.

Nisha let go of her hand. She signed at her. *How can you speak like me?*

Beth narrowed her eyes.

Sign. How sign?

Beth seemed to understand this. *Trying learn.*

Why?

For Granddad. Deaf now.

That's nice.

What?

That's nice.

Beth nodded.

Thought I was alone, Nisha said.

Beth looked at her sign. Shrugged. Nisha wished she'd remembered her school bag when she ran away. She'd left her pens and workbooks in there. Maybe Dad would be mad. They cost a lot of money. She didn't want him to have to pay any more.

But Beth started to sign again.

One day, I'll speak great. And help other people learn too.

Nisha felt a warmth in her chest. How had she known about this girl for years without knowing *this* about her?

You're nice.

Beth smiled. *Thank you. You too.*

Nisha smiled back.

And even though she'd seen so many horrible things, Nisha felt like she'd made a friend. Amidst all the horror, there was someone here with her who she liked. Maybe she could go to her house when all this settled down. Maybe Beth could come round hers. Maybe they could have tea together, those fish fingers Dad made best, and then maybe they could go watching films at the cinema and go to theme parks with Dad.

I don't many friend, Beth signed.

Nisha nodded. *Same.*

Friends?

Nisha felt her eyes getting heavy. *Friends.*

Beth smiled.

Nisha smiled back.

And in this silence, in the middle of all the dark things Nisha had seen, she felt warmth.

And then Beth's eyes rolled into the back of her head.

Her nose started bleeding.

And she fell down and cracked her head against the road.

DWAYNE

* * *

Dwayne saw Nico standing there, staring at him with those dead eyes, and he had a feeling getting off this road with his damned cash was gonna be even more difficult than it already was.

Nico stood there, staring at him. Or rather, through him. Right the fuck through him, with those dead eyes of his. *Was* he dead? Was that what this shit *was*? Some kind of zombie apocalypse? And what was it about zombie apocalypses where every time he read or watched stories about them, the people *in* the zombie apocalypse seemed blissfully unaware that zombie apocalypses were a *thing*? It was almost as if zombies weren't a mainstay of horror in the worlds those stories were set in.

But shit, why was he even thinking about bloody zombie apocalypse literature right now? Further up the street, a man was screaming as a crowd of these bastards—Gary included—mobbed him. He could hear car horns for miles. Sirens in the distance. Shouting. The smell of smoke. The taste of blood. And his body was burning after dragging himself out of the smashed rear windscreen, trying to escape.

But even worse than that, Nico.

Fucking Nico.

Dwayne held his rucksack of money. Nico might look pissed. Blood might be dripping down his face. And his eyes might look like they weren't of this world, to put it lightly.

But there was no way Dwayne was handing this rucksack of cash over. No chance.

For a moment, Dwayne wondered if this all might be some kind of almighty setup. Maybe this was some sort of elaborate plan from Nico and Gary to do a runner with the cash, to take it for themselves. Surely *that* was a more likely explanation than ACTUAL FUCKING ZOMBIES, right?

But Dwayne wasn't taking any chances.

He yanked the rucksack back. Ran to the left.

Nico grabbed him.

Pushed him back against the car with immense strength.

A splitting pain seared through Dwayne's back. Shit. It felt like he'd been stabbed again. Stabbed with glass. Shit. Broken glass. More broken glass. Middle of some kind of apocalyptic event and it was frigging *glass* that was going to be the end of it. How in the name of God was he going to explain that one to his mum?

Nico pressed Dwayne further back against the car. Dwayne tried to push him away. Tried to wriggle free. But he couldn't. He just couldn't. Dwayne was pressing him right back. Pushing him. Hard.

And his snapping jaws edged closer and closer...

Dwayne pushed hard against Nico. His heart raced. His hands shook. And even though he felt afraid for his life... it was still that bag of money he thought of. That rucksack of cash. Mum.

He held on to that rucksack. He wanted to protect it. He wanted to make sure nothing happened to it. He wanted to make sure he got it out of here, and then got away from here. First, Mum. Then, Spain. Simple as that.

Right?

Nico pushed harder against him. His teeth snapped, just inches from Dwayne's face. His breath was acrid. It always was, to be fair. But probably didn't help that he'd just bitten Gary's arm. Gary's sweaty arm.

He tried to kick Nico. Tried to trip him. Tried to upset his balance.

But Nico just kept on pushing.

And then he saw the others.

Gary.

The others.

Turning around.

Looking over at Dwayne.

And then running this way.

Shit.

Shit shit shit.

He held the rucksack. He clenched on to it. And he pressed up against Nico.

And he felt Nico's hands on the rucksack.

He felt him gripping it.

He didn't want to let it go.

He didn't want to drop it.

He didn't want to let Mum down.

But as he stood there, he found himself closing his eyes.

He found himself welling up.

Because he knew there was only one thing he could do.

"I'm sorry, Mum," he said. "I'm sorry."

And then he let the rucksack loose from his shoulders, and he wormed his way out of it.

He saw Nico tumble over. He saw the cash spill out of the rucksack. And he saw Nico's bloody prints, all over it.

All that cash.

All those chances of a new future.

All those opportunities for a fresh start.

Gone.

He closed his eyes.

He took a deep breath.

"I'm sorry, Mum."

And then he turned around and without thinking about it anymore, he did what he always did.

He put himself first.

And he ran for his life.

PETE

* * *

Pete stood at the edge of the motorway bridge looking down on the road, towards his and Helen's home, when he heard the blood-curdling whimper behind him.

Rain trickled down from above, refreshingly contrasting the suffocating heat. The road below was so clear in comparison to the motorway he was on. If he could just get down there, he'd hopefully have a fairly clear path back to Helen. Even though he was gasping. Even though he had a nasty stitch. And even though he wasn't sure how much further he could run.

He'd keep running. He'd keep going.

For Helen.

But that whimper.

"Help. Please. Help."

He heard that voice. A kid's voice. And it made him feel weird inside. Really weird. Because he couldn't afford to slow down. He couldn't afford to stop. And he couldn't afford to get sentimental in any way. Not for anyone. It was clear what he had to do now. His path ahead was clear. He had to get back home. He had to get to Helen. He had to make sure she was okay.

"Please..."

But that voice. That voice took him back to earlier today. To just before.

Opening that door.

Sacrificing that kid for his own life...

No.

No, he'd done that to survive. He'd *had* to do that to survive.

But now he had an opportunity.

Now he had a chance.

A chance to do something different.

A chance to make amends.

He turned around. Slowly. Even though his gut told him he needed to push forward. Even though instinct told him he needed to press on.

A boy sat inside a Land Rover. He had to be about nine, ten. Bright blue eyes. The lightest blond hair he'd ever seen.

And that pitiful, terrified expression on his face, as he sat there, teeth chattering.

"Help me. They took Mum. They bit her. Then she went away with them. And I need help. Please, officer. Please."

Officer. Pete looked down. He might've tossed his badge aside, but he still had his uniform on. He didn't *feel* like an officer right now. Sure as shit didn't.

But that's what he was, wasn't it?

He was a police officer. He was a protector of the law. He looked out for people. And it was his duty to help.

Shit. He'd been shameful. Running away from duty. Running away from duty when there were people out here in need.

He took a deep breath of the clammy air. Things were gonna be different from now on. He was going to be stronger. He was going to be *better*.

He looked over his shoulder. Over the motorway bridge.

Then he looked back around at the kid.

"Don't worry, son," he said. "I'm coming."

He started walking towards the car when suddenly he heard something up the road.

Something that made his stomach knot.

Something that made his chest tighten.

Something that filled him with fear.

When he turned around and looked down the road, he saw something that sent shivers right down his spine.

A group.

A group of people.

Running towards him.

He stood there. Frozen. The bastards. The ruthless bastards with whatever disease was taking over them. They were coming. They were coming for him, and he needed to get away.

But…

That kid.

That boy.

He looked at the rage-filled bastards running his way. Then around, at the kid.

Did he have time?

It was going to be cutting it close. But he had to have time. He had to believe he had time.

He gritted his teeth. Thought about turning away. That's what he had to do. Turn away. Go find Helen. Go find Helen, because she's depending on you. She's waiting on you.

And then, once again, in his mind's eye, he saw that little girl.

The one he'd left behind.

The one whose screams would haunt his nightmares—if he lived long enough to *have* another nightmare.

No.

He wasn't turning his back on duty again.

He gritted his teeth and he clenched his fists and he ran to the boy.

He reached the side of the car. Opened the door.

"Come on, kid. We need to get out of here. It's not safe."

The kid stared at him with wide eyes. "My belt. It's stuck."

"Stuck? What do you mean it's stuck?"

The kid pressed the seatbelt button. Nothing happened.

"Fuck," Pete said. "Sorry. Language. I…"

He tried the belt button himself. Tried pushing it.

But it didn't budge.

"Shit."

He turned around.

Those figures grew closer.

Eight of them that he could see.

All running wildly towards him.

All clearly suffering the same affliction as Colin, and Stan…

He reached for his pockets. For something he could use. Something he could use to help cut the belt away.

But he couldn't find anything.

"Shit!"

He looked around. Broken glass. That was it. A broken windscreen of the car beside him.

He ran over to it. Grabbed the glass. Tried to yank a sharp shard away from the window—

A sharp pain split through the middle of his palm.

"Fuck!"

That wasn't good. That wasn't good at all.

He stood there. Bleeding. Holding his palm. He couldn't break the glass free. And the kid was still in the car. Still attached by that seatbelt.

"Please," the kid whimpered. "Please."

Pete ran over to him. Looked back at the people running towards him, who were getting closer, and closer…

He looked at the kid.

Looked at him, as he struggled with that seatbelt.

"Please. Don't leave me. Help me. Please."

Pete took as deep a breath as his terrified body would allow. "Don't worry, kid. I'm here. I'm right here."

He saw a tear roll down the kid's face. Saw a spark in his eyes. "Really? You'll stay? You'll help?"

Pete's eyes welled up. Visions of Helen filled his mind. She wasn't answering her calls. No—someone *else* answered her calls.

"Sure," Pete said. "I'm right here. Right here."

He pictured the girl back on the road.

He pictured Stan.

He pictured Colin.

He pictured all the blood, and all the screams, and all the horror that ensued.

And then he heard that gasping and that growling, further up the street. Not far away now. Not long left. Ten seconds, maybe.

"Thank you," the boy said. "Thank you."

Pete looked at him.

He saw him smiling through his tears.

And then he shook his head.

"I'm so, so sorry."

The kid's eyes widened. "What—No!"

Pete slammed the car door shut.

And then he ran as fast as he could, towards the motorway bridge. Towards the trees beside it. Towards that drop that led down towards the road.

And as he ran away from the oncoming group of savages, he pictured that little boy in his head.

"I'll come back for you. I—I promise I'll come back for you."

And then Pete threw himself down the slope, and he cried.

DAVID

* * *

David crept through Mrs Kirkham's house and swore he heard footsteps creaking in the darkness.

All the curtains in this place were closed. It was dark, even though it was the middle of the day. The air was clammy and humid. Moths and flies flickered around him, butting into him. The carpet underfoot was uneven and dirty. Damn. And he gave himself a hard time for his place being a shit tip. *This* was how Mrs Kirkham was living? Poor thing.

Rufus walked close by his side. The wound on his back end didn't seem to be as bad as he first thought. It was kind of nice having Rufus here with him. Still didn't know where the hell he'd come from, and still didn't know what the hell he was going to do with him when he got out of here.

But right now, he was kind of grateful for his company.

He had to get out of this house. He had to find Keira. Hell, he had to get to the hospital first and hope to God Keira still worked there. That would be a start, wouldn't it?

With each step, the creaking floorboards reminded him of the fragility of his situation. He tried to make as little noise as possible, but the thick tension in the air seemed to amplify every sound he made. Sweat trickled down his forehead. His heart raced in his chest.

He focused on the front door. Tried to ignore the movement he swore he'd seen in the shadows when he first entered this house. And he tried to ignore the faint sound of banging outside. Mrs Kirkham. Mrs Kirkham, still powering on, still trying to stop him. It didn't make sense. It didn't make any damned sense at all.

And he got the feeling he was going to find out some answers first-hand, as soon as he got out of this damned house.

Or maybe he wasn't going to find out any answers. Maybe he was just going to stumble upon even more questions.

Screw it. As long as he got out of here, that was all that mattered.

He crept along the hallway. Saw the dust particles dancing in the air before him. His throat was dry. His chest was tight. And every single sound around him or movement in his periphery filled him with fear, making him even more tense.

He had this. He had this and he was going to get the hell out of this.

He reached the front door.

Placed his trembling hand on the cold doorknob.

A wave of relief crashed into him. He'd made it. He'd made it and he was one step closer to finding Keira. Whatever happened on the outside, well he could figure that out as it came.

But he was getting out of this house. He was getting out of here.

That was the first step.

He went to turn the knob, and then he heard something that filled him with terror.

Footsteps.

Creaking footsteps, right behind him.

He closed his eyes. Swallowed a lump in his throat. By his side, he heard Rufus, growling. Shit. Couldn't catch a damned break today, could he? Not just for one damned minute?

He lowered the handle.

Pulled the door.

It didn't budge.

Of course it didn't budge.

He didn't want to turn around. He didn't want to see what Rufus was growling at. And he didn't want to see the source of those footsteps.

Footsteps.

Slowly creeping towards him.

Step by step by step...

Visions of Mrs Kirkham filled his mind. Covered in blood. And that wound, on her throat. And then the news. The news of the riots, and the attacks at the hospital, and all the chaos out there.

And then, suddenly, a crippling thought dawned on him.

Who attacked Mrs Kirkham?

Who put her in the condition she was in?

His mouth drying up, David took a deep breath, and then he turned around. Slowly.

In the darkness, he saw the figure. He saw the nurse's uniform. He saw that necklace. That necklace dangling around this woman's neck.

And he saw her face.

She was pale. Her emerald green eyes glistened in the dim light. But like emerald, there was no life to them. No light to them. They were... empty.

Blood oozed down this woman's face. Dark red patches of blood stained her blue uniform. Her eyes, which were no doubt once caring, were now glazed over with a sinister emptiness. Her movements were slow and deliberate, and her outstretched hands were stained with dried blood—as were her false nails, two of them cracked, chipped.

David's stomach sank. She'd fallen victim to whatever horror plagued the world outside, too. She was the one who'd attacked Mrs Kirkham. Her nurse. The health visitor who came to see her regularly. She'd attacked Mrs Kirkham. And now she was here, right in front of David.

Fear clenched David's throat. But he refused to let it paralyse him. He stepped back, Rufus by his side, preparing himself for whatever lay ahead.

And then the nurse lunged at him with surprising speed.

Her mouth twisted into a grotesque snarl.

Instinct took over David. He sidestepped her attack, narrowly avoiding her snapping jaws.

His mind raced, searching for a way to defend himself. He spotted a nearby umbrella by the door. He grabbed it. Wielded it, like a makeshift weapon. Not the best, but it would have to do. With a surge of adrenaline, he swung it at the nurse, striking her with a resounding thud.

She stumbled back, momentarily stunned.

Taking advantage of the momentary reprieve, David raced into the kitchen. He searched the drawers. Every drawer. Keys. Keys. He just needed some bloody keys.

A gasp filled the kitchen. He turned around and saw the nurse flying across the room, towards him.

He sidestepped her again as Rufus whimpered at his feet. And then he ran back into the hallway, took a left into the lounge. He slammed the door shut, and he looked around this lounge. The windows, heavily curtained. The bed in the middle of the room. The stack of television magazines, almost as high as the ceiling.

The window.

The open window.

He heard banging against the lounge door. Saw Rufus, cowered, tail between his legs. Whimpering.

"Come on, lad," David said. "Just another few steps. Just another..."

Then the door slammed open.

David grabbed Rufus by his collar.

He dragged him towards the window.

He picked him up. Flung him outside, even though he didn't want to hurt the dog.

And then he clambered out the window, squeezing himself through it, as the nurse snatched at his ankles and grabbed him and—

He fell out of the window.

Hit the ground.

And then he reached up and slammed that window in her face.

The nurse scratched at the window. She bit at the glass. Her glazed eyes peered out into nothingness, as blood transferred from her lips onto that dusty glass.

David breathed heavily. He leaned against the garden wall, trying to steady his racing heart. Rufus cowered at his feet.

"It's okay, lad," David said, stroking his fur with his shaking hand. "It's—it's okay now."

He looked back up at that woman. At the necklace dangling from her neck.

The dog necklace. Remarkably like a golden retriever.

And he saw the uniform. The nurse's uniform. And he thought of Keira.

And as he patted Rufus, he knew he had to press on.

He had to navigate whatever treacherous path to the hospital awaited him, where his daughter's fate remained uncertain—if she was even at that hospital at all.

With Rufus by his side, he steeled himself for whatever challenges lay ahead, determined to find Keira and keep her safe, no matter the cost.

He turned around, and he walked towards the nurse's car.

KEIRA

* * *

Keira sat with her back against the rear of the lift and listened to the echoing commotion outside.

The dim light flickered above. It was going to go out eventually. Keira just knew it. It was going to go out, and she was going to die in here, this metal tomb. Every now and then, she looked over at Nitesh, who sat beside her. Caught a fearful glance. She could see how afraid he looked. She could see the weight of hopelessness pressing down on him, confining him from all four corners. And she knew she probably had that same look of fear in her own eyes.

The lift's polished interior reflected her anxious expression. She tried not to look at it, but she couldn't help gazing into space. The creaking elevator machinery punctuated the silence, and added to the tension. Keira's heartbeat thumped loudly in her ears. The distant echoes of chaos filled the lift, a constant reminder of the danger surrounding them.

The faint scent of antiseptic that always lingered in the hospital was even stronger in this confined space. Mixed with it, an unmistakable metallic tang of fear, permeating the air. And the subtle aroma of Nitesh's cologne, and the faint hint of coffee on his breath. A nice cologne. Nothing too offensive. Fresh. Almost comforting amidst the uncertainty.

Keira felt the cool, smooth surface of the lift's metal walls against her fingertips. Beside her, Nitesh's warmth, adding to that sense of reassurance, even though their predicament was completely shitty. She felt the slightest of vibrations, and the gentle swaying of the lift, a constant reminder of their trapped state.

Keira's mouth was dry. A subtle aftertaste of green tea from earlier mixed with the tang of blood. She felt... sick. Isolated. Lost. Trapped.

"I never did like taking the lift," Nitesh said.

And Keira did something weird when he spoke. Something unexpected. She laughed.

"What's so funny?"

Keira shook her head. "Nothing. I just... We're trapped in a lift. We're probably never going to get out. We're probably going to suffocate to death, because oxygen's gonna run out eventually. And here we are, talking about likes and dislikes."

"That's life, isn't it?"

"Yeah," Keira said. "That's life."

Nitesh took a deep breath. Sighed. "I just wish I'd had a chance to propose to Dina. Before... before all this."

"I'm sure you'll still get that chance someday."

Nitesh turned to her. Glared. "Really?"

"No. Probably not. We're probably going to die in here."

Nitesh nodded. "I appreciate the honesty."

"Good. Not everyone does."

She turned around. Stared at that cold metal again. "I watched a man who should've died rise to his feet. I watched him tear a young doctor apart. And then I saw my friend. My friend, bitten.

Mobbed. And I couldn't do anything to help. For my friends. For my patients. For anyone."

"You helped me," Nitesh said.

"Huh?"

"I'm here. I'm alive. You helped me."

"You're trapped in a lift because of me."

"And I would've been torn apart if it wasn't for you. I was in the midst of a panic attack. It's thanks to you that I'm still alive. So cheers. Cheers for delaying my death. For making it somewhat less painful. Long, and drawn out, sure. But surely less painful than what's happening to the people out there."

Keira nodded. She sensed a sincerity to Nitesh's words. A genuine gratitude to them. Maybe she had failed Jean. Maybe she hadn't been able to help her friends. But he was alive. He was alive because she'd helped him. Wasn't that exactly what she was on this planet to do?

Nitesh reached into his pocket. Pulled out a bag of Murray Mints.

"Wow," Keira said. "I haven't had a Murray Mint since I was about twelve."

"Good memories?"

"Not especially. They remind me of my dad."

"You should be grateful of your parents. Not all of us get the chance to appreciate them while they're around." He popped a Murray Mint in his mouth, and he crunched down on it immediately. The noise went right through Keira.

"I'll appreciate whoever I want," Keira said. "Appreciation is earned. He never earned it."

"I'm sorry to hear that," Nitesh said. "But... well. If this is the end, I do hope you'll be able to make peace with the past. You'll die a lot more honourably if you do."

Keira laughed again.

"You do have a dark sense of humour, don't you?" Nitesh said.

"I suppose I do."

He smiled. Looked away. "I lost both my parents in the Iranian revolution. They managed to get me away with Auntie. They weren't so lucky."

"I'm sorry."

"I never appreciated the sacrifice my parents made for me until they died. I was ungrateful. Because I didn't understand how fortunate I was, to have the life I had. But I've never forgotten their sacrifice. I've never stopped appreciating them. To this day."

He looked at Keira then, with tear-glazed eyes.

"My wife. She's sick. My daughters. They need me. And I'll give up anything for them. I'd sacrifice everything for them."

He turned around again. "I don't know what happened between you and your father. But whatever happened, I hope you're able to make peace."

Keira felt a heaviness to the air. A weight to her chest. Those words. Those words about making peace. Maybe it was everything she'd been through today. Maybe the shock, settling in.

But there was something about those words that made her think of Dad, and made her eyes water. Made her throat swell. And made her bottom lip twitch.

"My family are right here," Keira said. "Here in this hospital. And as long as I'm alive, I'll do what I can to protect them. No matter what."

Nitesh looked right into her eyes. Smiled at her, warmly. "I hope that brings you…"

And then out of nowhere, a sudden jolt shook the lift.

Keira grabbed Nitesh for support, instinctively. And he grabbed her too.

"What…" Nitesh started.

But there was no doubting what was happening.

The lift was sparking back to life.

The digital numbers flickered down until they hit GF. Ground Floor.

A moment's silence. A moment's pause.

Keira looked at Nitesh.

Nitesh looked back at Keira.

Neither of them speaking.

Both holding their breath.

Both still.

And then, in the silence, a piercing ping filled the lift, and the doors creaked open.

NISHA

* * *

Nisha watched Beth collapse to the road.

Beth crumpled before her. The strength drained out of her body right away and she fell to the ground. Just like that, she dropped down. She was standing one moment, and then she was on the road. No. No. This couldn't be happening. Not Beth. Beth was her friend. Beth couldn't collapse. She couldn't have anything happen to Beth, too. Or she'd be alone. Completely alone.

Nisha reached down and she shook Beth's shoulders. Beth's skin felt cold and clammy. She touched her face, not knowing what to do. Her skin felt weird. She didn't move. She didn't move when Nisha touched her. She just flopped there, lifeless. Eyes closed. Not like when Dad was asleep, and she jumped on him to wake him up and he laughed and chased her around the house—hide and seek was extra scary and extra fun when you were deaf.

She didn't move at all.

Nisha's mouth turned dry. She smelled something like pennies in the air, and sour, too. She held on to Beth's shoulders. Shook her. Her heart raced. The butterflies in her tummy flapped their wings harder than ever now. Please, Beth. Please wake up. Please come back. Please wake up.

But she didn't feel like Beth was coming back.

She didn't feel like Beth was coming back at all.

Instinctively, she started signing to Beth. *Wake up. Please.* And then she realised how stupid she was being. Beth was unconscious. She wasn't awake. She was lying here and it didn't matter how much Nisha signed to her, she couldn't hear what she was saying. Couldn't hear her at all.

She looked up at the road. Saw the cars. Saw the houses. She saw movement in the distance, way ahead. But she couldn't do anything to get their attention. She wasn't even sure she wanted to get their attention. Because they could be bad people. Bad people, like the people at the school.

She looked back down at Beth. She felt warmth on her face. Tasted saltiness on her dry lips.

Please, Beth.

Please.

She saw Beth's smile just moments ago.

She felt that warmth she'd felt, when her and Beth said they were going to be friends. That they were going to face whatever other horrible things lay ahead of them today, together. She thought they were going to get home and this was all going to settle down and they'd soon be back at school, only best friends now; friends who did things at the weekend, friends who went out for food and to the cinema, friends forever.

But Beth was still.

Nisha stared down at her. Tears dropped down from her eyes, onto Beth.

Why?

Why?

And then, just like that, Beth's eyes snapped open.

For a second, Nisha felt the butterflies in her belly stop flapping. Her eyes were open. She was okay. She was going to be okay.

But then her heart sank.

Her eyes were just like Ginger Harry; just like Mrs Thompson's. They were just like the eyes of all the other angry people she'd seen. Like they weren't really looking at her. Like she couldn't really see her.

Beth. Please no. Please.

She wanted to sign to her. She wanted to speak to her. She wanted Beth to just tell her she was okay. That everything was okay.

Before Nisha got the chance to pull her arms back and sign, Beth lunged up at her.

Nisha lunged back. She pushed Beth away. Her heart raced as she staggered back, towards a car.

Beth's face. That look on her face. And those marks on her arm. The marks of blood she wasn't trying to hide anymore.

She was bitten. Like the others.

And now she was one of them.

Nisha shook her head as Beth stood there, opening her mouth, like she was screaming at her.

She lifted her shaking hands.

Please, Beth. It's me. Friend.

Beth looked at her hands as they wafted through the air. Maybe that's all Nisha needed to do. Maybe Beth would understand. Maybe her eyes would go back to normal and she'd smile and they'd laugh about it and get ice cream and be happy.

But Beth just flew towards Nisha.

Nisha stepped aside from Beth. She watched as she hurtled into the car door; as she fell face flat across the back seats.

Nisha stood at the door. Shaking. She held the door. Beth lay there, writhing around. Blood splattered from her lips and her eyes. She wriggled around like a worm, trying to get out.

And Nisha didn't want to hurt Beth. She didn't want to hurt

her new friend. Because this was Beth. She was still in there, somewhere.

Beth turned around. Her neck snapped right back. She looked into Nisha's eyes.

Nisha held up her hands again.

It's me. I won't hurt you. It's me.

Another pause.

Another moment of hesitation.

And then Beth came flying towards her.

Nisha slammed the door shut.

Beth's face cracked against the window. Nisha winced. She'd banged her head right against it. That had to hurt. It had to hurt and she felt so bad for her.

She stood there. Tears streaming down her face. She saw that car door between her and Beth. That window, a barrier between them both, like the barrier of the television screens that always stood between her and her favourite people. She saw Beth's eyes and she tried to see something human in there. Something that made her open the door. Something that told Nisha she was okay again. That everything was okay.

But Beth just clawed and scratched at the window.

Nisha watched the car rock and shake. She pressed her hand against the glass, then took it away, her fingers leaving little smudges on there, which Beth slammed her hands against. And Nisha felt heavy inside. Nisha felt sick inside. Nisha wanted Dad. She wanted Beth. She wanted home.

She stood there, and she took a step back. She didn't want to walk away from Beth. She didn't want to leave her friend.

But she needed to find Dad.

Because Dad was the only one who'd know how to help.

Dad always knew how to help.

But would he know how to help this?

She swallowed a lump in her throat.

She held up her fingers, and she waved them through the air, as she looked right into Beth's eyes.

I'm sorry.

And then she turned around, and she walked away, into the endless silence.

DWAYNE

* * *

Dwayne leaned back against the wall and buried his head in his sweaty hands.

The alleyway's graffiti-covered walls loomed around him, their vibrant colours faded, chipped, and decaying. Broken glass and scattered rubbish littered the ground. Distant sirens wailed in the background, a constant reminder of the chaos and unrest plaguing the city. A rat scurried across the pavement, its tiny claws scraping against the concrete.

The pungent smell of garbage lingered in the air, mingling with the dampness of the alley. From the distance, a faint scent of smoke wafted through the air, intermingled with the unmistakable stench of decay from a nearby bin.

The rough texture of the graffiti brushed against Dwayne's fingertips as he leaned against the wall for support. Beads of sweat trickled down his forehead. The bitter taste of regret lingered on his tongue. A familiar lingering taste of disappointment, tainting his every thought.

He'd managed to escape Nico and Gary, and get off the road.

But he'd lost all his stolen money in the process. He rubbed his trembling fingers through his sweaty, greasy hair, struggling to breathe. The weight of his failures pressed down intensely on his sore shoulders. He'd failed. He'd failed Mum. Just like he always failed her.

He pressed his shaking fingers against his face. This was supposed to be her way out. This was supposed to be *his* way out. And now Nico was dead? He looked infected with something beyond recognition. Definitely didn't look like he was springing back to life any time soon.

And the money was gone.

A heavy sigh escaped his lips. His shoulders sagged. If he'd taken a proper career, he wouldn't be in this mess. If he'd listened to his mum, worked hard at school, he wouldn't be in this position, right now. And neither would she. He wanted to help her. And he'd failed her. He'd...

But wait.

The chaos. All this chaos, unfolding around him.

As much as he wanted the money—as much as it was everything to him—what if he didn't *need* the money anymore?

A flicker of hope replaced the resignation. He saw the consequences of his actions before him. He saw the selfish path he'd chosen, and the position it'd put him in. He saw the hurt he'd caused. The pain he'd caused. He saw Brighton...

No. Not Brighton. Not now.

But in the midst of all the loss, Dwayne saw something else.

A chance.

An opportunity.

Because if the world really was going to shit all around him, then maybe it wasn't the end of the line after all.

He stood up. Took a deep breath. Looked down the alleyway, back towards the road.

He was going to get to the care home.

He was going to find Mum.

And he was going to get her out of there, if it was the last thing he did.

He took another deep breath, and he stepped out of that alleyway.

By his side, he saw the school, and somewhere in the distance, he heard the desperate wails of a girl...

PETE

* * *

Pete stopped walking when he reached the top of his road, and he took a deep breath.

The sun beamed down on the cracked lane. The overgrown trees, filled with bright green leaves, stretched over the road. Birds sung overhead. In the distance, sirens echoed—but they were far enough away that he didn't have to worry about them here. He took a deep breath. Smelled the freshness of the air. It contrasted the city's air so much—that clammy, exhaust-tinged air. One of the main reasons he loved this place so much. It was such a nice place to call home.

He missed it.

He missed it a lot.

His mouth felt dry. The taste of vomit crept across his tongue. Memories of the road darted before his eyes.

Colin.

Stan.

The girl he'd used as a distraction.

And then the boy he'd left behind.

A sinking sensation welled up inside him. The boy. He'd left him in that car. Looked him in the eye, and told him he wasn't going to leave him. That he was going to stay there with him.

And then...

And then he'd ran away.

Pete squeezed his eyes shut. His ears rang. He shook his head. He'd done the only thing he could. Because Helen was in danger. Helen needed help. His wife needed help. He couldn't just leave her.

And he was going to go back for the boy. He really was. As soon as he found Helen, he was going to go back out to the motorway and he was going to save that boy. He was going to drag him out of that car and he was going to take him away with him. He'd look after him. Raise him as his own, if that's what it came to.

Fuck. What was he even on about? This shit wasn't going to last. It might be bad now, but the government would sort it. Right?

Shit. The *government?* The same government who'd partied their way through successive COVID lockdowns? The same government who'd crashed the economy on a whim? *That* government?

Yeah. Maybe his faith was misplaced.

He took a deep breath and he looked down the road. It was a country lane, so it was always quiet. Right now was no different. His heart raced. A bitter taste crossed his lips. He was home. He'd made it home. He'd made it to Helen? Hopefully. Hopefully.

But at what cost?

He felt his jaw clenching. He swallowed another lump in his throat.

He'd made it this far. Family first.

And once he found Helen—once he knew she was okay—*then* he could focus on making amends for the things he'd done.

Then he could focus on being a police officer.

He walked down the road. Walked past the tall hedges. He walked down the slope he always used to enjoy running down, back in the good days. Back in the summer sun. Back when things were good. When things were exactly how they should be.

He climbed up the other side of the hill and he saw the bridleway on his left. He'd walked down that bridleway so many times. It wasn't a million miles away from civilisation. But down there, down that bridleway, he used to feel like he was in the middle of nowhere. Like he was truly alone. Alone with his thoughts. A million miles away from *everything*.

He reached his house.

He stopped, right in front of it. Held his breath. His stomach churned up with the memories. The white paint still needed another glossing over. Ivy crawled up the side of it, clambering its way into the side window. So many memories. So many good memories. Didn't matter how long he spent away from this place. This was home.

He walked down the drive. Retraced those steps he'd walked a thousand times. He walked up to the door. Grabbed the handle. He pictured turning that handle. Pictured turning it and walking in and finding Helen in there, hiding, afraid.

He pictured holding her. Comforting her. Telling her everything was going to be okay. That he was here now, and he was going to look after her. Everything was going to be okay again.

He went to turn the handle.

The handle didn't budge.

Locked. Of course it was locked. It was always bloody locked. Helen didn't like being in on her own. She didn't like the thought that someone could just wander in with an axe and rip her to shreds, or something like that.

He reached into his pocket. Pulled out his key. Put it in the lock, and turned it.

The lock didn't turn.

Wait. That wasn't right. This was his front door key. It should work. It *definitely* should work.

He tried turning it again. Tried rotating it.

But again, nothing.

It didn't budge.

He stepped back. Looked at the window. The curtains were closed. She could be dead in there. Or alive in there. Alive, and suffering.

That voice. That *man's* voice, on the phone.

"Don't call us again."

Who was that?

And what had he done with Helen?

He loved this house. This was his home. This was the place he'd felt the most comfortable in his life. More so than his childhood home. More so than *anywhere*.

And he hated the thought of damaging it.

But right now, time was of the essence.

Right now, he knew he only had one choice.

He grabbed a loose brick beside the door.

He pulled it back.

And then he smashed the window apart.

Glass shattered everywhere, filling his lounge. He scrambled over the shards of glass, tumbled inside the lounge. He had to hurry. He had to be quick. Helen could be in danger. She could need help.

"Helen!" he called, shooting back to his feet. "It's okay. I'm here now. I'm..."

And then he saw her appear, right there in the kitchen doorway.

Standing there. Wide-eyed. Pale. Just as gorgeous as he remembered when he last saw her.

"Helen," Pete gasped. "It's okay. You're okay now—"

"Pete?" she said. Her voice quivering.

"Yes," Pete said, taking a step towards her. "It's me, Helen. It's me. It's all going to be okay now. It's all…"

And then she said the words that broke Pete's world into pieces, all over again.

"What the hell are you doing in my house?"

DAVID

* * *

David managed to get a good few miles out of the car before it ground to a sudden halt.

The car was absolutely boiling hot. Outside, the sun shone down brightly, creating a greenhouse effect in here. Abandoned cars filled the roads. On his right, a bus lay on its side, its front wedged into an overturned lamppost. David heard screams. Sirens. The sounds of panic. The sounds of chaos. All around him. And he found himself realising that this shit was even worse than it looked on the news. And it looked pretty frigging bad on the news for starters.

The air reeked of exhaust fumes. A slight metallic tang pierced the air. And a sickly sweet tang covered David's lips, making him feel shitty as hell. Beside him, he heard Rufus panting, as he sat there, tongue dangling between his teeth. The wound on his back wasn't bleeding anywhere near as much anymore. That was something, at least. And the fact that it was a bite mark and it wasn't leaking blood, too? Yeah, that was another bonus.

Because as much as he didn't have a *clue* what was happening here… there was clearly something to the bites. Something that *spread* in the bites. He didn't know that was a thing. He didn't know that was possible. Shit, nothing about today was possible on paper, was it?

But here he was. Sitting in a broken-down car that didn't even belong to him—it belonged to the nurse that he'd left locked in Mrs Kirkham's house. And he'd taken it without permission. And it'd run out of petrol. Of course it had. Of course it bloody had.

He saw the cars ahead. And he saw the hospital in the distance. He was close. So close. But the mass of cars around this place, it was terrifying. He could see smoke rising from the hospital, too. And as he sat here in the driver's seat, he got the feeling that he was heading right towards something he didn't want to find. Towards something dangerous. Something he should steer well clear of.

But… well, Keira. She worked at the hospital, as far as he was aware. And as long as she was there… he was gonna fight to find her. They might not have been the best of pals over the last few years. But she was his daughter. She was his kid. And he'd do goddamned *anything* to find her. To protect her.

He went to climb out the car when he noticed something, dangling from the rear-view.

A picture. A picture on a keyring. The nurse. And Rufus. Shit. So he was her dog. And she'd *bitten* him? Poor dog. Poor damned soul.

David looked at Rufus. Initially, he kind of thought he was gonna have to let Rufus go, as soon as he knew he was pretty safe.

But right now, the thought of leaving him… yeah, that didn't sit right with him. It didn't sit right with him at all.

Rufus stared up at him. Panting. Ears raised.

David took a deep breath, and he sighed. "Come on, you. Figure we'd better get out of here, hadn't we?"

He opened the door. Rufus hopped out alongside him.

And then he stood in the middle of the road.

David took a deep breath, and he walked. He made his way cautiously through the eerily silent streets, stepping over debris and broken glass as the hospital inched closer. This once bustling road now lay desolate, lined with abandoned cars that seemed frozen in time. What the hell had happened here? And why did it feel like everyone had abandoned their cars to head *to* the hospital —*to* the place he was heading?

Some vehicles were crashing into one another, their metal frames twisted and broken. Others stood solitary, doors ajar, as if their owners had fled in a hurry.

Shit.

He stepped closer to the hospital, Rufus by his side. The closer he got, the more chaotic the scene before him grew. Thick plumes of dark smoke billowed from the building, reaching up towards the ashen sky. The acrid smell of burning filled the air, stinging David's nostrils, making him cough involuntarily. The crackling sound of flames intensified, creating an unsettling symphony of destruction.

There was an unsettling feeling in the air. A sense that things could spiral out of control on these streets at any given moment. That the silence could be filled at any second with screams, with shouts, with chaos.

He gritted his teeth. He was so close to the hospital now. Part of him didn't even *want* to see it. Because that part of him feared what he might find there—and what it might mean.

He walked past the final abandoned cars, and he saw it.

The hospital's once pristine facade was now marred by broken windows and charred walls. Flames surrounded it, dancing and devouring everything in their path. The glass entrance doors stood shattered, their remnants scattered across the ground like broken shards of hope. The emergency lights flickered intermittently, casting eerie shadows on the surrounding chaos. Ambulances filled the car park. Doctors and nurses raced out from the flames and the smoke, patients by their side. Blood splattered the concrete. So much chaos. So much panic. So much confusion.

David swallowed a lump in his throat as he stood there, looking out over this entire scene. He stood there. Shaking. Rufus by his side. He listened to the screaming. Listened to the sirens. And he saw the panic unfolding right in front of him, and the realisation sunk deeply into his body.

If Keira was here, working at this hospital, then she was in even bigger danger than he first thought.

KEIRA

* * *

The lift doors parted, and Keira braced herself for whatever she was about to witness in the surreal scene before her.

Keira's eyes widened. The hospital's main entrance lay in ruins, the once sturdy doors now reduced to splintered fragments, scattered across the floor. Flames flickered and danced in the distance, casting an ominous glow that illuminated across the chaos ahead. The shattered glass of the main entrance reflected the dim light from the flames, and thick plumes of smoke billowed in the air, making it hard to see.

The acrid stench of smoke mixed with a hint of burning plastic and chemicals filled her nostrils. The hospital was on fire. The hospital was on *fire*. It was going to burn down. It was going to burn down, and everyone inside was going to end up trapped here.

They were going to die here.

A faint, metallic tang of blood lingered in the air, too. A

sombre reminder of the events unfolding right before her. And a stench she'd never forget.

The rush of warm air carrying the faint heat from the distant flames brushed against her face. She gripped the lift handrail tight, grounding herself in the midst of the turmoil. The flames crackled and roared in the distance, an unsettling symphony echoing through the emptying corridors.

And so too did the sound of a nurse's panicked voice, as she ran past. "The kids! They're—they're stuck in there! They're trapped."

Keira turned around to the children's ward. Shit. The nurses and the doctors were abandoning this place. Fleeing this place. They were giving up. And the children's ward... it was too far away. Too dangerous to reach.

They were giving up on the kids.

Keira's mouth was dry. A metallic tang crossed her lips. Blood. And the very taste of adrenaline itself, as her heart raced with the weight of the decision she knew lay ahead.

She saw the doors. She saw the flames. She saw the smoke. And she saw an opportunity. She saw a chance. A chance to get out of here. A chance to get away from this place. A chance to escape.

And she didn't know what awaited her outside. By the looks of things, nothing good.

But anything was better than being trapped in here.

Anything was better than dying in here.

"We need to go," Nitesh said. "There's nothing we can do."

His voice cracked. Tears rolled down his cheeks. She could see how conflicted he was, just looking in his eyes.

"There's nothing we can do," he said. "We have to save ourselves."

Keira looked at the doors leading down the long corridor towards the children's ward.

And then she looked back at those broken double doors at the front of the hospital. She couldn't just walk away. She couldn't just abandon her duties here. She couldn't leave.

She took a deep breath of that smoke-tinged air. Torn between preservation and the duty she felt towards the vulnerable patients in the children's ward. She thought of Omar. Of Jean. And of what Jean made her promise.

To find Omar's daughter.

To protect her.

And as she stood there, the shouting and the screaming growing louder around her, the flames getting hotter, the taste of blood growing more metallic... she felt the overwhelming gravity of the situation absorbing into her bloodstream.

She needed to make a choice.

She needed to make a sacrifice.

She turned around to Nitesh. Put her hands on his shoulders.

"Save yourself," she said. "Save your family. Your daughters need you. And your wife needs you."

Nitesh shook his head. Tears fell freely down his face. "You can't do this—"

"I can," Keira said. "I don't have anyone relying on me like you do. Only the people here. The children here. And I'm not leaving them behind. I'm not letting them die. So you go. You save your family. And I'll do everything I can to save these kids."

Nitesh shook his head as the flames grew hotter, as the smoke grew thicker.

"Go!" she said.

Nitesh lowered his head. Looked at the ground with wide, defeated eyes.

"I'll remember your kindness," he said. "I'll remember your sacrifice. And I'll make sure I find my children. I'll make sure I protect them. And when you get out of here... *when* you get out of here... you'll make amends with your father. You promise me that."

She looked into Nitesh's eyes. Her vision grew hazy. Her eyelids grew heavy.

"Thank you," he said.

And then he turned around and ran away.

She watched him. Watching him running down the corridor. Watched him tumbling over the fallen litter. She watched him scramble around patients, helping them, and then running over towards that broken glass, as the flames and the smoke grew thicker.

And then she saw him turn around and look her right in the eye.

He looked right at her. Nodded.

And she nodded back at him.

And then he turned around and ran out of the hospital.

Keira stood in the lift. She took a steadying breath, as she stepped forward, crossing the threshold of the open lift doors. She walked over to the children's ward. Screaming echoed through the corridors. Heat filled the hospital. The smell of burning grew stronger, stronger.

She stood at the door to that children's ward corridor, and she swallowed all the doubts, and all the fear, and all the terror inside her.

And then she pushed that door open, and stepped into the corridor.

It was time to do what she was here to do.

Protect those in need.

Duty over everything else.

NISHA

* * *

Nisha was lost.

She could see smoke in the distance, over by the town centre, which was actually a city centre but for some reason everyone still called it "town." And that made her stomach feel a bit upset. Because if there was smoke rising from town, then the horrible things she'd witnessed back at school must be happening there, too.

And the horrible thing that happened to Beth.

To her friend.

She walked along the pavement. It was cracked and rough, worn down. She kept looking ahead at all times, but she wasn't sure she wanted to see any more horrible things. Things even worse than the scary movies Dad watched on his own at night, with the monsters, and the blood, and the screaming. Nisha didn't understand why he watched those films. He told her it was just entertainment. Just special effects. She didn't care. It was still creepy and scary and she didn't like it.

She smelled smoke. And that smell after it'd rained on a warm day, too. She used to like that smell. It smelled like soil. Like leaves. But after today, she wasn't sure she'd ever like that smell again.

Because it would always remind her of school.

Of Beth.

She walked down the road and wondered how to get back home. She had to take a long way round, because she saw some of the bad people before and got scared, and now she thought she recognised this road but she wasn't sure. It always looked different when she was with Dad. It never looked this scary when she was with Dad.

She thought about Beth. Maybe she could go back for her. Maybe she could find her. Maybe she'd be okay now. Maybe everything would be okay now, and they'd both be okay together.

But she'd watched Beth turn. Watched her turn into one of those bad people. One of those monsters.

And she knew there was no way Beth was safe to go back to.

And even if she wanted to, she didn't even know where to go.

She saw something up ahead, then. A road. A little shop on the left that she recognised. Yes. This was a road she knew. And if she could make it down this road, she could make it home. She could make it to Dad.

And then she saw the swarm of people up ahead, their movements frantic and disorganised, like they were dancing in pain. Some of them stumbled and fell over, their hands reaching out for help. Others frantically fought back, swinging handbags, prams, everything, some of them clutching children close.

The shop on the left that sold nice sweets that Dad always bought Nisha was all smashed up. The smell of burned rubber filled the air, and mixed with the smoke, making Nisha feel sick. And there was blood all over the concrete.

Nisha's heart sank. She saw the people running away and she knew that this horrible world was getting even worse. She couldn't go down the road. Because there was something bad down there. Something dangerous down there.

So where was she supposed to go?

She turned back. Running. Because even though she couldn't hear them, she could see them getting closer, *smell* them getting closer. They were going to get her. They were going to catch up with her and they were going to get her because she was weak. She was too weak. She wasn't strong enough. She couldn't fight for herself. She was too weak and...

More figures.

More of them running in that weird way, right up ahead.

Running towards her.

She stood there. Frozen. She wrapped her arms around her chest. They were going to get her. They were going to get her and Dad wasn't going to come to help. No one was going to come to help. They were going to bite her and they were going to make her bleed, just like the kids in the classroom, just like Mrs Thompson, just like...

She felt something, then. Something nudged her, right behind her. Made her swing around and let out a cry.

And then she saw someone.

A car pressed right up against her. It looked an old, rusty car. Blue, once, but all covered in bird poo and rusty metal.

A man waved out the window. His lips moved. And he looked like he had a little smile on his lips. She couldn't tell what he was saying. But he was pointing towards the back of the car with his thumb.

She saw the figures in the distance. And then she saw them to her side. And even though Dad told her to never trust strangers, to never talk to strangers... if she didn't get in this car, she was going to die. That's what was going to happen. She was going to die. Or even worse. She was going to get as sick as everyone else. And everyone was so, so sick, and scary sick too, not just like when Nisha was sick and her tonsils were sore and they gave her ice cream to make them feel better.

She took a deep breath and as much as she didn't want to, she ran to the back of the car. She grabbed the door. Opened it. Looked over her shoulder, and saw them. A ginger man, with a hole in his leg, bleeding. A little woman, naked, and covered in nasty teeth marks. And an old man, with anger in his eyes, all running towards her.

She didn't know what this was. She didn't know what was wrong with everyone. It was a dream. It was a nightmare. It had to be.

But she threw herself into the car, and slammed the door shut. And the car started to move.

Nisha took deep breaths, trying to calm herself down. And as the car moved, the butterflies flapped around her tummy again.

The man looked over his shoulder at her. His mouth moved, but she couldn't tell what he was saying. He was thin, lanky, and even though everything was awful outside, he was smiling. His face was pale, and a few greasy strands of hair dangled across his forehead, but the rest of his head was bald.

He looked from Nisha to the road and then back again. There was something off about him. Something that made Nisha feel sick. He looked nervous. Sweaty. Shaky. But happy at the same time. And it just made Nisha feel all weird.

And the car. The car itself. The seats were all worn and stained. It looked such an old car. A weird smell hung in the air, like her cousin Sammi's hamster cage when her hamster died. Strange objects cluttered the dashboard—a cracked doll with empty eyes stared back at her. A small jar filled with some kind of weird little creature sitting in green liquid. And a bunch of faded photographs, curled and brown at the edges.

A shiver ran down Nisha's spine as she looked at the driver. As she saw that smile on his face again.

He turned around. Faced the road.

She reached for the handle. Tried to turn it.

The door was locked.

The driver looked back at her.

His lips moved.

And then he smiled.

Nisha might be safe from the outside.

But it was the man she was trapped inside with that she was afraid of now.

DWAYNE

* * *

Dwayne ran as fast as he could towards Mum's care home and hoped to God he wasn't too late.

All around him, everywhere he went, chaotic scenes of distress and confusion followed him. People rushed by, their faces filled with fear and desperation. Flashing lights of emergency vehicles flickered in the distance, and plumes of smoke rose into the sky from afar. The air reverberated with a cacophony of sounds. A clamour of terrified voices. The distant wails of sirens pierced through the air. And every now and then, tires screeched against the road as cars tried to navigate the chaotic streets.

He kept his focus on his footsteps. Tension filled his muscles. Sweat trickled down his forehead. Smoke filled his lungs, as well as burning debris, constantly reminding him of the danger and chaos surrounding him. A metallic tang covered Dwayne's lips. He had to move quickly. He had to get to the care home. He had to be there for her, before she fell victim to whatever plague was taking over this city. He might not have the money. But he was *here*. And he was going to get her out of there and look after her. He'd let her down enough in his life so far. He wasn't going to let her down anymore.

He stared down the long road. In the distance, he saw people running down the next street, looking over their shoulders. A mother and child tumbled over, and the crowd just ploughed over them, scrambling over their fallen bodies, no-one stopping to help; everyone looking out for themselves. Shit. Is that what things had come to? Is that how far humanity had sunk in just one damned day?

But then Dwayne was hardly an angel, was he? He'd used someone as bait earlier. His conscience was hardly clean.

He turned away. Walked down the road, towards the pub. He could cut through the car park. Get to the road behind the pub near the old council estate, and then the care home would be just a short way down there. He was close. So close. And yet it felt like he was still a million miles away.

He thought of Mum. Her wide eyes, staring up at him. That confused smile, etched across her face. "What are we doing, Dwayne? Where are you taking me?"

And where *would* he take her? She'd sold her house to partly fund the care costs. And then she'd burned through all those—or rather, *he* had burned through all those, as her guarantor. And that's why she'd ended up in shitty care. A care system she couldn't escape. A prison of Dwayne's making.

He was just trying to create a better life for himself, so that he could give *her* a better life.

But it backfired. It failed. Again, and again, and again.

He didn't want to tell Mum his living arrangements. He didn't want to tell her he lived in hostels. And that some nights he lived on the streets. It was only a makeshift thing. Only a stopgap. Eventually, he'd find his own place. That was the plan. Costa del Sol. A house in the sun. And the best care Mum could ever hope for.

He ran down the road. Saw the pub on his right. Movement twitched in the corner of his vision. Don't turn around. Just focus on the path ahead. Just keep going. Just...

He couldn't explain why. But movement caught his attention. Down the road. He had no idea why *this* movement caught his attention over any other.

But when it did, he turned around.

A little girl, no more than ten years old, getting into a car parked in the middle of the road. A rusty old Toyota. A bloke held a hand out, pointed at the back door.

A pang of recognition struck Dwayne. Was that...? Shit. It *was*. Harry. Pedo fucking Harry.

What the hell was he doing out of prison already?

And what the *hell* was he doing ushering a little girl into the back of his car?

He remembered Pedo Harry well. Proper creep, as the nickname suggested. Former schoolteacher. Seemed a pretty ordinary fella, until he kidnapped three kids one day. The details of what he did to them... yeah, that shit was too grim to even think about.

And the worst thing about it? He had the easiest ride in prison. Separated from the rest of the prisoners. Lived with the rest of the sex offenders and nonces. And sure, every now and then, someone got to him—he got hot water laced with sugar tossed at his face once, but unfortunately it missed, and he got off the hook. Easy ride.

And now here he was. Driving a car. And inviting a little girl into the back of his car, as a group of manic strangers ran down the road towards the car from afar.

A knot tightened in Dwayne's stomach. Harry was a monster. He had to be stopped. Taking advantage of a kid while the city went to shit around him? Yeah. That was a special kind of messed up. And it made Dwayne sick.

He looked at that car, and the little girl standing beside it. Then he looked at the figures approaching the car. And then he looked over his shoulder, at the quiet, empty remains of the old pub. A shiver crept down his spine. The thought of what might happen to that girl. The horrible thoughts of what might happen to her, at the hands of that monster.

But then...

Mum.

Trapped in that care home.

Time ticking away.

And every moment he wasted was another moment where she could be plunged into further danger.

He stood there, torn in two directions. Finding Mum. And the moral obligation he felt to protect this child. His eyes darted back and forth. Mum or the kid? Mum or the kid? Time stood still. Both choices were dangerous. Both choices were painful. Both choices were...

He stood right there, in the middle of the road.

He looked at the car.

Then at the pub.

He swallowed a lump in his throat.

He knew what he had to do.

He knew *exactly* what he had to do.

Dwayne took a deep breath.

And then he walked.

PETE

* * *

"Pete? What are you doing here?"

Pete stood in the middle of the lounge of the place he still called home, to this day. The same worn-out furniture decorated the room. Faded wallpaper peeled off the walls, a job he always promised he'd finish. Where pictures of him and Helen used to sit on the mantlepiece, there were new pictures now. Pictures of Helen, yes. But also pictures of someone else.

Silence enveloped the cottage as he stood there, staring into Helen's eyes. Distant sounds of chaos filtered in from outside, a constant reminder of the world beyond these four walls. The air in the cottage carried a musty scent, a lingering fragrance of aged books, and the warmth of the wooden floorboards, heated up in the sun. A crippling chasm of emptiness opened up, right in the middle of his chest. The nostalgia. The memories. So many memories. He tasted saltiness, and he realised he was crying.

And amidst this time capsule of nostalgia, right in the middle of it... Helen.

Her eyes widened. Her body shook. "What are you doing here? In my house?"

Pete took a step towards her. "It's okay, Helen. You don't have to worry anymore."

Helen staggered back. She scrambled into her pocket, pulled out her phone.

"Who are you calling?" Pete asked.

"The police. You shouldn't be here."

"Oh, Helen, stop this."

"Stay away from me," she said, scrambling with her phone.

"Helen, I'm here because I want to help—"

"Stay the fuck away from me!"

Her words echoed around the lounge of the cottage. A reminder of the arguments they had, towards the end of their marriage; at the breakdown of their relationship. Begging her. Begging her to give him another chance. Begging her to give him another chance to prove to her that he loved her, even after everything he'd done.

She lifted the phone to her ear. Whimpered. And then she lowered the phone again, and looked right up at Pete. "I'm begging you," she said. "Not now. Not with everything going on. Save yourself, Pete. If you've got any respect for what we once had... save yourself. Please."

Pete opened his mouth when he saw a shadow appear at the door.

A man. Bald. Big beard. Well-built guy. The sort of guy who ran his own mortgage broker business, probably. The sort of fella who was a member at the local tennis club, and had loads of toff mates that he drank with on weekends.

"What's happening here?" the man asked.

Helen stared at Pete. Her eyes were wide. And Pete sensed danger. He sensed *she* was in danger. He sensed that she needed protecting. She needed looking after. She needed defending. From whoever this man was.

"What's happening here is I'm having a conversation with my wife."

"Pete," Helen said.

The man frowned. "Your *wife?*"

"Billy, I—"

"Oh," the man—Billy—said. His eyes widened. The confusion slipped from his face. Suddenly, a smile crept across his lips. "Oh, I get it. I see who this is. The uniform. The face like a slapped arse. You must be Pete. We've never had the pleasure of meeting."

He walked over to Pete, slowly. His footsteps cracked against the broken glass underfoot. He held out a hand. Confident. Unmoving. "Billy."

Pete looked down at Billy's outstretched hand. So this was Helen's new piece? Disgusting. No way was he shaking his hand. No way was he being *patronised,* right in the middle of *his* house.

Billy lowered his hand. Stepped back. "Fair enough. I figure the last few years have been rough for you. Losing the love of your life, and all that."

"Billy, please," Helen said.

A fire ignited in Pete's chest. His lounge. His house. His wife. And this smirking prick thought he had the better of him?

"You've made quite a mess of our window."

"It's my window, actually," Pete said.

Billy smirked. "That's right. You still have a stake in this place, don't you? Just a shame your assets are tied up with Helen's so much, and you'll never see a penny of it."

Pete felt his jaw tensing. Keep it calm. Keep it cool. Don't flip. Don't let the bastard goad you.

"So what're you doing here, anyway?" Billy asked. "The world's ending out there, and you're... here? This place isn't your home. Don't you have someplace else to be?"

Pete looked at Helen. She looked back at him. And he felt that void between them. That chasm between them. But also that bridge. That bridge that had always existed between them.

"I'm here for you, Helen. I'm here because I'm going to look after you. I'm going to protect you. I'm going to be better than I was before. I promise."

Helen lowered her head. Looked down at the wooden floor.

And then Billy laughed.

He planted his hands on his thighs. Laughed so much he keeled over, started spluttering. "*You're* going to look after her? *You're* going to protect her? And how the hell do you think that's gonna work, eh?"

Pete's face turned hot. He wanted a hole in the ground to open up and swallow him. This was a nightmare. This was a bad dream. And he wanted to escape it. He wanted to get away.

Billy walked up to him. Squared up to him. "How the hell do you ever expect to look after her when you couldn't even protect your boy?"

Those words.

Like daggers to Pete's chest.

Billy turned around. Walked away, walked towards Helen. Saying something. Saying things under his breath.

But Pete didn't hear him.

All he heard were those words.

When you couldn't even protect your boy?

He saw the brick in the middle of the floor.

He saw the brick, and he saw Billy, and he felt all his embarrassment, and all his inadequacies, and all his pain, and he saw all the violence on the outside, all the horror on the outside, all of it replaying in his mind.

And then he reached down and he grabbed that brick.

He pulled it back.

Walked over to Billy.

And then he cracked it over his head.

Hard.

Billy tumbled to the floor.

Helen screamed.

Billy turned around. Looked up at him. Blood leaked from the side of his head. His left eye twitched, bulging out of his skull slightly more than the right.

"What..." he said. Blood spluttering out of his lips, and onto the wooden floor.

And Pete knew he should stop.

Stop.

This wasn't him.

He wasn't a violent person. He was a police officer. He protected people. He looked after people.

He...

You couldn't even protect your boy.

"Pete!" Helen screamed. "Please! Pete!"

But Pete couldn't stop.

He crouched down.

Raised that brick higher.

The violence outside flickered in his mind's eye.

And then he cracked it against Billy's head.

Hard.

He pulled it back again. Swung it at Billy's head. Kept on swinging, and swinging, and swinging, as more blood splattered up onto his hand and his arm, as Helen screamed and cried, and as all of his embarrassment and all of his shame of the last few years dissipated, all in an instant.

And then he stopped.

He sat there. Shaking. He looked down at Billy. Or rather, where Billy's head used to be. Those eyes, sitting in a soup of skull fragments and mashed brain. The chunks of hair clinging to that brick in his hand.

And Helen, standing above them both, gasping, wailing.

Pete stood up.

He walked over to Helen.

She tried to get away, but he grabbed her.

Grabbed her with his bloody hands, and held her, close.

"You don't have to worry anymore," Pete said. "I'm here now. I'm home. And you're going to be okay. I'm going to look after you. Everything's going to be okay."

DAVID

* * *

David ran down towards the hospital and tried not to think about the flames, and the smoke, and the screaming.

Flames flickered beyond the broken glass of the main entrance. Sirens echoed from the ambulances, battling to line up at the front of the hospital. A paramedic sprinted past, fear in his eyes, abandoning his duty. On the side of the pavement, two more paramedics crouched over an old man, giving him CPR, battling to bring him back to life.

The hospital was always a pretty chaotic place. But right now, it was more chaotic than David had ever seen it. The flames. The smoke. The cries. And the knowledge of the horrors unfolding far beyond this hospital. Mrs Kirkham. Mrs Kirkham's nurse. So much horror. So much chaos. So much... loss.

He thought about the news. The news of the riots. Of the attacks. And of the hospitals going to shit. It seemed like the hospitals were the absolute epicentre of disaster. Cause everyone flocked to the hospital in times of need.

But right now, it was clear to David that the hospital was the last place anyone wanted to be.

He just had to hope Keira wasn't here.

And if she was, he just had to pray she was safe.

He ran up to the smashed windows in the main entrance. People staggered out, sprinting away. Flames crept across the walls. Smoke filled his lungs, making him splutter. Shit. Where did he even start? Keira used to work as a nurse on the main wards, didn't she? But there were a shitload of main wards. And none of those main wards looked particularly accessible right now.

So what in the name of hell was he supposed to do?

He looked down at Rufus. He tucked his tail between his legs. His ears drooped beside his head. A little whimper crept out of his mouth. He didn't look happy, poor guy. He'd just been attacked by his owner, ended up wandering along with another bloke on a journey, and now he was expected to wander into a collapsing, burning hospital with that guy? Nah. Nah, that wasn't right.

A nurse ran past. Ginger hair. Tears streaming down her cheeks.

"Excuse me," David said. "Do you know—do you know a Keira Watson?"

But the nurse just ran past, wailing.

David stood at the door. He felt sick. Those flames, they were climbing higher up the walls. The smoke grew more suffocating, more intense. The window of opportunity for entering this hospital was rapidly disappearing.

"Keira Watson," David shouted. "Does—does anyone know Keira Watson?"

No one responded. Just shouts. Cries. Sirens. And confused screams.

"Keira Watson?"

A voice. Right beside him.

He swung around.

An Asian man stood before her. He had kind eyes. He looked right at David.

"Did—did you say—"

"Keira Watson," the man said. "The nurse. From ward 32?"

Ward 32. That sounded high up. But shit—Keira Watson. He knew Keira Watson. Which meant she worked here. She worked here. So there was still a chance he could save her. There was still a chance.

"Where is she?" David gasped. "What do you know about her?"

The man turned around. He looked through the broken glass of those double doors.

David grabbed the man by his collar. "Tell me where she is. Tell me where she—"

"She stayed back to help the children. But the children's ward. The flames. They're already too high. And the smoke's already too thick."

David turned around. Keira. She was so caring. So thoughtful. Always was. Always had been.

He looked in through the entrance. Through the smoky haze, towards the flames.

"Where is the children's ward?"

"It's already too late—"

"I didn't ask you whether it was too late or not. I asked you where it is?"

The man hesitated, for just a moment.

And then he raised a shaking finger.

"On the right of the lift."

David turned around. On the right of the lift. So that was where he needed to go. That's where he needed to go to find her. That's where...

And then he saw them.

The flames.

The smoke.

Right in front of that door.

Right in front of the door the man was pointing towards.

"I'm sorry," the man said. "I tried to tell her. I tried to tell her it was too late already. But..."

And then all his words faded into the darkness.

Because Keira was in this hospital.

Keira was behind that flame-covered door.

Keira was already gone.

But no. He couldn't just accept that.

He ran. Ran into the hospital. He ran towards the flames. He felt the smoke fill his lungs, burn his throat. But he kept going. Kept stumbling through the main entrance area, Rufus barking behind him, the man shouting after him. "Please! Wait!"

David ran over to the door. A wall of flames. And an even thicker wall of smoke.

He tried to run through it. He tried to run around it. He tried to force himself to plough through it.

But it didn't matter how much he tried. David could only stand there, and stare through that little pane of glass, and into the smoke-filled horror beyond.

Keira was in there.

His girl was in there.

And there was nothing he could do to help her.

KEIRA

* * *

Keira stepped onto the children's ward and the scale of the decision she'd just made hit her like a bus.

Flickering emergency lights cast eerie shadows across the ward. Furniture lay overturned on its side, and medical supplies lay scattered across the floor. Up ahead, she saw frightened children huddled together, their faces etched with fear and confusion.

Distant wails and screams echoed through the corridor, as the crackling flames consumed the air.

"Please," the children begged. "Help us. Please help us."

Smoke filled Keira's nostrils. Shit. She had to be careful. She had to hurry. If she didn't hurry, she was going to die of smoke inhalation. She could smell whiffs of antiseptic, too, and the metallic tang of blood, mingling with the burning odour. It sent a shiver down Keira's spine.

A dryness filled Keira's mouth. She was gasping for a drink. And the anxiety of the situation wasn't helping, either. A thin layer of sweat trickled across her lips, as the oppressive heat emanated from the surrounding flames, warming her skin and making it difficult to breathe.

She had to focus.

Focus on the scene ahead.

"Don't worry," Keira shouted. "I'm here. I'm here to help you."

Keira ran into the ward. All the children in here were out of their beds, crouched together. The beds were in flames. They were trapped. Trapped inside here. And if Keira wasn't quick, they were going to be swallowed up by the heat completely.

"Come on," she said. "Let's get out of here."

As she turned around, she saw a wall of flames and thick smoke blocking her way out. Shit. Those flames had grown even higher since she barged through the door. She wasn't going to be able to get through there. She was going to have to find another way.

Out of nowhere, a gasp filled the air.

The children's eyes all widened. Fear crossed their faces.

And Keira knew why.

She turned around.

Slowly.

Down the corridor, right at the bottom, more shouting. More gasping. More of those possessed moans and wails.

The infected. They were here.

And they were getting closer.

Keira ushered the kids down the corridor. "We need to get out of here. Stay close. I'll find a way."

She looked at that door. The flames were too high.

The windows were all locked. And they were all barred up. Who the hell put metal bars in a children's ward? Shit. What was she going to do? What the hell could she possibly do?

The crying inched closer. Footsteps hammered against the hospital floor. Shadows flickered in the distance, approaching this ward.

Keira's stomach turned. She looked around everywhere for a

way out. No way through the door she'd come in through. No way out of the windows. Not a single damned fire extinguisher on display.

And no way through the path of infected hurtling down the corridor towards her, either.

What was she going to do?

She looked around. Heart racing. Focused on the task at hand. She wasn't leaving these kids behind. She wasn't failing them. They were her patients, and this was her hospital, and this was her duty. This was her life.

She looked around everywhere when she saw it.

A skylight.

A skylight over on the extension of the ward. The smoke creeping towards it, seeping out of it.

If smoke was seeping out of it, then that meant...

It was a way out.

A potential way out.

Hope sparked inside her. She ran down the corridor, with the kids. "Come on. Stay close. You look at me, okay? Keep your eyes on me."

She reached the skylight and a new problem presented itself. How was she going to get up there? It was too high. Way too high. She needed something to stand on. She needed a bed, or a...

Across the corridor, she saw a chair.

She ran over to the chair. Grabbed it, almost tumbling in the process.

And then she heard another scream.

Right at the bottom of the corridor. Way, way down this endless corridor. She saw it.

The woman.

The woman, standing there, covered in blood.

Staring at her.

One of *them*.

And then, the next thing she knew... more of them joined her.

Stood there for a second.

Stared at Keira.

And then raced down the corridor towards her.

She turned around and dragged the chair towards the skylight. Just stay focused. Just stay focused on what you've got to do. You're gonna be okay. You're gonna be—

She dropped the chair. Lost her footing.

Shit!

She took a breath, and regretted it 'cause the smoke inhalation burned her lungs. She grabbed the chair, lifted it, and then ran down the corridor again. Towards that skylight. Trying not to focus on the approaching infected. Trying to just focus on that skylight, and these kids, and this way out.

She planted the chair under the skylight. Stood on it. Reached up, tried to bash the skylight away.

It didn't budge.

Another scream echoed through the corridor. Beneath her, a little boy whimpered. "I want my mummy."

"It's okay," Keira said. "I'm going to get you out of this. I'm going to get us all out of this. I promise."

She bashed against the skylight. Kept on punching. Kept on hitting it.

But still it didn't budge.

She closed her burning eyes. Her body shook. Defeat flickered in her mind. Omar. Gavin. Jean. And so many patients. So many dead patients.

But...

No.

She opened her eyes.

Looked up at the skylight.

She was getting out of here.

And she was getting these kids out of here, too.

She pulled back her fists and she bashed the skylight as hard as she could.

It cracked. Crumbled down onto her, raining down shards of plastic.

But she didn't care about that. There was a way out. There was a chance.

She stepped off the chair and saw the figures hurtling down the corridor.

They were still far away. But... but they were getting closer. And Keira had five kids here. Was she going to get them all out in time? How the hell was she going to get them all out in time?

Shit. No point dwelling on it. Less dwelling, more *doing*.

"Come on," she said, grabbing the first kid and then stepping onto the chair, a little girl with a bald head and a pale face. "Up through the skylight here. You'll be safe up there. I promise."

The kid shook her head. "I'm scared."

"I know," Keira said. "But there's no time to be scared right now. Trust me. Please trust me. We'll get you out of here."

The kid looked like she was going to resist again.

And then to Keira's relief, she nodded.

Keira lifted her up. Almost did her back in doing so. Held out her arms for the next kid, a little boy.

"Come on. I'll get you out."

She lifted the boy. Then lifted the next boy, and then the next girl. And then there was just one left. A little girl.

Down the corridor, she saw them. Close. So close. Two women leading the charge. Blood oozing down their chins.

She looked back at the kid. "I've got you," she said.

And then she reached down. Grabbed the kid. Lifted her up to the skylight, as smoke filled her lungs, made her wheeze, and as the dizziness surrounded her, and...

The kid grabbed onto the skylight.

Dragged herself out.

Looked down at Keira.

"Thank you," she said.

Keira nodded at her. Smiled, as tears stung her burning face. "You'll be okay. You'll be okay."

And then the kid disappeared.

Keira stood there in the thickening smoke. The flames crawled across the floor and the walls. And the screaming infected lunged closer, closer...

But as she stood there, crying, she felt proud.

She'd done what she had to do.

She'd saved the children.

And whatever happened next... at least she knew she'd done what she was born to do.

She'd cared for those in need.

She'd—

And then the chair wobbled, tumbled underneath her feet, and she fell and cracked her head on the floor below.

NISHA

* * *

Nisha sat in the car and she wished she'd listened to Dad's advice never to get into cars with strangers.

Her heart pounded in her chest. She couldn't stop shaking. The car smelled weird, like something rotten. She remembered when Dad found a dead rat by the garden shed, once. That smell, so strong, making her feel sick, making her feel dizzy. It smelled a bit like that in here.

Was that what the classroom would smell like soon? Was that what the bloody remains of all her friends would smell like?

Or were they all going to rise up, just like Ginger Harry? Like… Beth?

She could smell cigarette smoke too. And that smell like Dad had on his breath when he'd had alcohol when he was sad about Mum. She didn't like that smell. She loved Dad, but she didn't like him when he'd had the alcohol. It made him even more sad, and it scared Nisha.

So she'd go to bed. She'd lie there and she'd pretend she was asleep. And when he came in during the night, when he stroked her hair, she lay so still and let him. Because he was sad. He was sad about Mum, and she made him feel better.

Her cheeks burned. Sweat trickled down her forehead. Vibrations rumbled through her body, as the man steered the car down roads she didn't know; roads she didn't recognise. And everywhere they drove, Nisha saw more trouble. She saw people running down the road, trying to get away from something. She saw bodies lying on the side of the road, covered in blood. She saw dogs racing down streets, tails between their legs, fear in their wide eyes.

But she wanted to be out there more than she wanted to be in this car right now.

She turned around. The man stared ahead, driving. His mouth moved, but Nisha couldn't hear what he was saying. She could smell his sour breath from here. His eyes stayed focused on the road ahead. But every few seconds, he looked up in his mirror and stared right at Nisha.

Like he was checking if she was still there.

So Nisha waited. She sat very still in the back of the car and she waited.

Waited for him to look up into her eyes.

And when he did... she knew what she had to do.

She held her breath. Her heart pounded.

Just wait.

Just be brave.

Just...

The man's eyes peered in the mirror at her.

His lips moved.

She held his gaze. Looked right into those eyes.

And then he looked back at the road and she knew she had to try something.

She reached for the door handle. Grabbed it. Pulled it.

But the door didn't open.

Her stomach sank. It was locked. Of course it was locked. Bad men like him didn't leave their doors unlocked. She was trapped. She was stuck in here and there was nothing she could do. There was nothing she could...

She turned around.

The man's eyes stared right at her again. Only they didn't look as happy now. They looked... bloodshot. Bloodshot and angry.

He turned around. His eyes widened. He opened his mouth and he shouted something at her. Flecks of spit splattered against her face.

And then he smiled.

Smiled, and turned back around to the road.

Nisha froze up. So it wasn't just a bad feeling. This man didn't want to help her. This man was bad.

She didn't know what bad men did to kids. But she knew Dad told her never to get into a car with someone she never knew. And she knew some of the other kids teased each other's parents too. Nonces, or something, a word one of them wrote down on a piece of paper and handed to Nisha one day. *Your dad's a nonce.* Nisha thought it was a nice thing maybe, 'cause who could ever think a bad thing about Dad?

But then she took it home to Dad and showed him and he told Nisha it wasn't a nice thing. And that she shouldn't say that to anyone else. When she found out it was a bad thing and searched for it online, she realised why Dad didn't want to be called that.

Maybe she'd call Connor Best's dad that one day.

She'd never get the chance to. Not now.

She reached for the handle at the other side of the car. This one didn't move either. Her heart sunk. A cold shiver ran down her spine. She couldn't escape. She was trapped here.

The man glanced up in the rear-view mirror again. He looked like he was laughing this time. A nasty smile grew across his face. Why was he smiling. What was he so happy about?

And then he turned down a road that looked quieter than the

rest. A car park. An empty car park. The concrete was covered in glass. There were empty beer bottles everywhere. It didn't look a nice place at all.

He stopped the car. And then he sat there a few seconds. Lips moving, but Nisha unable to hear what he was saying.

And then he turned around.

His eyes stared right into her. A smile crept further up his face. He put a finger over his lips.

Nisha couldn't move. She was frozen solid. The doors were locked. The windows were too strong to break.

She was trapped.

And then the man reached into his pocket.

He kept his hand there a few seconds.

His smile widened.

And then...

He pulled out a knife.

A shiver shot down Nisha's spine. Her belly ached, and she felt dampness around her bottom, like when she wet the bed at night. She couldn't move. She couldn't get out of here. She was trapped. She was trapped and she couldn't get out.

And then the man moved his finger away from his lips, and he smiled, as saliva drooled down his chin.

Nisha was trapped.

She was in danger.

And there was nowhere to run.

DAVID

* * *

David stared through the broken glass of the children's ward corridor door and he felt his whole damned world falling apart.

Smoke filled his lungs, making him cough, splutter, gag. Flames rose up the front of the door, and filled the corridor beyond. Screaming filled the hospital. Sirens blared out front. And somewhere behind him, a dog barked. Rufus. Rufus needed him.

But... Keira.

He thought about what that man told him. That doctor, by the door.

She'd gone back. She'd gone back to help the kids on the children's ward.

But the children's ward was now in flames.

The children's ward was in flames, and he couldn't just leave her here.

He stepped forward. Reached for the door.

Sharp pain split across his right arm. Heat. Pure, intense heat, burning him. The flames. The flames, searing his skin, making him wince.

Shit. He needed to get through this door. He needed to get in there. And he needed to find Keira. He couldn't leave her in there. He had to find her. He had to help her.

He'd failed her for far too many years. He couldn't fail her now, when she needed him most.

He reached out for the handle again. And again, a splitting, burning pain, right in the middle of his right hand.

He wanted to keep holding that handle. He wanted to find the courage and find the strength to push that door open, and step into that corridor.

But instinctively, he pulled back. Clutched his burning arm. Bit his lip, gritted his teeth, bent over and screamed.

Burning tears stung his eyes. More pained screams filled the corridor. The smoke grew thicker. David spluttered, the air growing hotter, more intense.

But Keira…

He lifted his head. Looked through that door. The door looked blurry, shimmering. Smoke, heat and tears.

And as much as he wanted to walk towards that door, as much as he wanted to push it open and press through and search for Keira and find her, as much as he wanted her to fall into his arms, and to carry her away, out of that corridor, saving her life… there was nothing he could do.

"Please," he gasped. "Please…"

And then he noticed something. Over to his left. A fire extinguisher. Flames danced across the walls beside it. Smoke billowed, blocking his view.

He had to get to that fire extinguisher.

He had to reach it in time.

And then he had to help Keira.

He ran over to the fire extinguisher. Flames stretched across the walls. The room grew hotter. The air grew thicker.

"Come on," David gasped. "I can do this. I can save her."

He ran as fast as he could across the corridor, eyes firmly set on that fire extinguisher.

He just had to get to it before the flames did.

He just had to get to it before...

An intense, burning tickle, right in the middle of his chest. He tried to breathe, tried to inhale. But he couldn't. He couldn't.

He coughed. Spluttered. Hurled his guts up all over the hospital floor. The smoke inhalation. It was getting stronger. It was growing harder to breathe.

He closed his burning eyes. Took the first deep breath he could—a gasp for whatever air was left in this waiting room.

And then he lifted his head and went to make his final push towards that extinguisher.

And then he froze.

The extinguisher was covered in flames. Flames crawled all over its surface, swallowing it up whole. His chance. His opportunity. It was gone.

He stood there. Shaking. Weak. And feeling dizzy.

He looked at that flame-bathed extinguisher.

And then he looked over at the door to the children's ward.

The flames.

The smoke.

And...

Behind it, David saw something.

Movement.

Keira?

He took a step towards it. He couldn't see properly for the smoke and the tears in his eyes. And if it was Keira... he wasn't sure he wanted to find her. He wasn't sure he wanted to see her, trapped in there. He wanted to believe she'd got away. He wanted to believe she'd escaped.

But he walked towards that door, no control over his motor functions, like someone was controlling him on a video game.

And then he saw them.

The figures. The faces. Men. Women. Burning.

Scratching at that glass.

Biting at that glass.

Trying to get out.

A knot tightened right in the middle of his chest. Mrs Kirkham. He couldn't stop thinking of Mrs Kirkham. And then of her nurse. And how they looked like her. How these people looked just like her.

And then, in his mind, he saw Keira.

Keira, just as he remembered her, when she was younger.

Covered in blood. Covered in bites.

Covered in...

He closed his eyes. The flames grew hotter. The smoke, thicker. Dizziness. Dizziness intensifying. Light-headedness. And the hotter he got, the more he felt like he was on holiday. Like he was on a beach, with Keira, and with Rina. The sand between his toes. Her laughter, right beside him. And Keira, splashing around in the water. *Daddy, look! Look at the wave I made!*

He thought of the good times, he thought of the memories, and he smiled, as tears rolled down his cheeks, and as those infected bastards banged on the door in front of him.

"I'm coming for you," he said. "I'll find you. I won't give up. I won't ever..."

And then, out of the chaos, in the midst of all the destruction, David heard a voice.

A voice that changed everything.

"Dad?"

NISHA

* * *

Nisha sat in the back of the car and her heart raced as the man held the knife and pointed it right at her.

She couldn't move. Her legs were wet. She could smell wee. Strong wee. And she knew it was herself. But she didn't feel embarrassed. Not like when she'd wet herself in assembly, and everyone laughed at her. She just felt scared.

Scared about this man.

Scared about what he was going to do to her, with that knife.

His lips moved. Saliva trickled down his chin. His breath stunk of death. She couldn't hear him. She couldn't tell what he was saying. In a way, she wasn't sure she wanted to. Wasn't sure that was a good idea. Because maybe he was saying bad things. Maybe he was saying horrible things.

And she didn't know whether she wanted to hear those things or not.

He smiled. He pulled back his knife. His lips started to move again.

Nisha reached for the door handle. Pulled it. But it didn't move. She was stuck. She was trapped. She was—

And then he grabbed her.

He grabbed her and he held her throat and he pushed the knife against her neck.

And as he held her with that tight hand, she felt so scared. She felt so afraid. She wanted Dad. She wanted Dad so much.

And then she saw something.

Movement. Movement in front of the car. Someone was here. Someone was here to help. Maybe the police. Maybe the army. Someone good was here to help her, and...

And then she saw them.

She saw the man, banging against the window.

She saw the blood.

And she saw his teeth, biting at the glass.

And that look in his eyes.

That empty look in his eyes.

Like Mrs Thompson.

Like Ginger Harry.

Like Beth.

The bad man turned around. He grabbed the steering wheel. Nisha saw him swearing. And then the man drove the car back, away from that man, and then spun around him. Maybe this was another chance. Maybe this was another chance for her to get away. Another chance for her to escape.

She tried the doors again. And then she tried the windows. One of those winding ones. And then she realised yes, she wasn't trapped. The window. The window was turning. The window was opening. She could get out of here. She could get out.

She turned that window turner. She rolled the window down as the car powered on. She could do this. She was strong. She could get out of here. She could get away.

She rolled the window down further and then she dragged

herself over to it and dragged herself through it and looked down at the moving tarmac below and—

A hand.

A tight hand, around her ankle.

She kicked back. Kicked the man right in his face.

His grip loosened.

And then Nisha tumbled out of the window, and onto the road.

The road smacked against her face. That metal taste of blood filled her mouth even more. She lay there, shaking, crying. She needed to be strong. She needed to get up and she needed to run and she needed to get back to Dad. She needed to—

Then someone turned her over. Onto her back. And again, for a moment, she found herself hoping it was Dad. She found herself praying it was someone nice. Someone good.

But when he turned her over, she saw him looking down at her, that smile on his face, and she knew it wasn't good at all.

The bad man. The driver.

Standing over her.

Smiling.

Holding that knife.

His lips moved, twitched. She couldn't tell what he was saying. But she thought she could make out that last word. And it made her insides freeze.

Dead.

He pulled back the knife and she squeezed her eyes shut and waited for the pain and prayed for Dad and...

And nothing happened.

No pain.

No feeling at all.

Nothing.

She lay there in the silent darkness, eyes squeezed shut.

And then when she'd been waiting for longer than she knew, she opened her eyes.

There was a man standing over her. But it wasn't the man from the car. The bad man.

It was someone else.

He was tall. Dark-haired. His skin was a bit dark, too. He had a beard, and slicked back hair, like the movie stars.

And he was holding out a hand, to Nisha.

She looked at that hand. Looked at the blood splattered against it.

And then beside her, she saw the bad man.

Lying there.

Rolling around.

Clutching his bleeding head.

Nisha looked back up at the man standing over her. He didn't look like police. He looked like a normal person. Or not a normal person. Maybe another bad person. Another bad man.

He pulled his hand away. Reached into his pocket. And Nisha's tummy butterflies flapped away again because maybe he had a knife too, maybe he was dangerous too, maybe he was going to hurt her too.

And then he pulled out his phone.

He tapped the screen. Maybe he knew Dad. Maybe he was calling Dad. Maybe he was going to get Dad here, and maybe everything was going to be okay.

But then he turned the screen around to Nisha. Held it in front of her face.

It took her a few seconds to see, through her blurry eyes, but she saw the words on the screen, and she felt a weight lift inside her.

My name is Dwayne.

You don't have to worry.

She looked at the screen. Read those words. Then looked up at this stranger—this Dwayne.

And in the silence, in the fear, even though he was a stranger, there was something about him that felt familiar. Something about him that made her feel safe.

He held out his hand again.

She looked at it.

Shaking.

Heart racing.

And then she saw the figures in the distance. The figures running down the road. Running through the buildings.

She was scared. She was afraid. She didn't know who this man was. She didn't trust him. She didn't trust any strangers.

But she saw those figures approaching, and she knew what she had to do.

She took the man's warm hand.

He looked down at her. Nodded. Half-smiled.

And then together, they ran.

KEIRA

* * *

"Dad?"
She saw him standing there in the flames. The smoke surrounding him, engulfing him. And at first she thought she was seeing things. She had to be seeing things. This shit had to be in her head. 'Cause there's no way Dad could possibly be here right now. He wouldn't come after her. He didn't even know if she still worked here. She hadn't spoken to him in years.

But when he turned around and looked into her eyes, she was a little girl again. A little girl lying in bed, listening to him tell her bedtime stories about lions and witches and wardrobes; a little girl walking hand in hand with her father, into the pouring rain; a little girl besotted by her father, who she idolised more than anyone else.

And then there were the later years. The years after Mum.

The way he changed.

The way she grew apart from him.

But seeing him there, sweating, covered in blood, coughing

and spluttering with the heat and the flames, all of those later years disintegrated; went up in smoke.

Because Dad was here.

"Keira?" he gasped.

Keira turned to Nitesh, who stood with the kids she'd helped escape the children's ward. Almost died in the process, but just about managed to drag herself out.

He nodded at her. "You do what you have to do." This dog, right by his side.

She nodded back at him.

Turned around to the hospital.

Took a deep breath of the fresh air, before the smoke surrounded her.

"I'm coming for you, Dad," she said. The last patient. The last patient she had to save. "I'm coming."

She ran inside the hospital. A wall of heat battered her immediately. Smoke seeped right in through her nostrils, making her cough and wheeze. Her eyes stung. Her legs shook.

But she had to keep going.

Dad needed her right now.

"It's okay," she gasped. "I'm coming, Dad. I'm—I'm here."

Dad limped through the hospital entrance area. The waiting area was in total disarray and ruin. Flames everywhere. Seats overturned. Smoke, getting blacker and blacker. And somewhere from deep within the belly of the hospital, the sound of people crying. Screaming. The ones who hadn't been so lucky as to get away.

She ran towards Dad. Kept on running. He staggered further forward. Off balance. Weak. Almost passing out with the smoke exhaustion.

But she wasn't letting that happen.

She wasn't letting him die in here.

She ran right over to him and then she grabbed his hand.

She felt that tension, as he grabbed her back, as he held her for support. She felt that sense of resistance, swelling up inside her. The distance. The detachment. And the discomfort she had with any sort of closeness.

And then she held him back. Purely for support. "Come on," she said. "Let's get you out of here."

She ran, holding Dad, back towards those broken hospital doors.

Then, out of nowhere, right behind her, she heard a door bang open. A chorus of skin-crawling groans filled the waiting area. Crap. Was that what she thought it was?

She didn't want to look over her shoulder. She didn't want to look back.

But instinct took over.

Two of them. Two of those bastards she'd narrowly escaped from the children's ward. They'd managed to bash the door down. And now they stood there, flames crawling up their bodies, staring right at Keira. Right at Dad.

Keira spun around and ran. She couldn't think. She didn't have time to think. She just turned around and ran, as those groans grew closer. Turned around and ran, as their footsteps edged nearer, and nearer, and at least she was holding Dad's hand, at least Dad was here now, at least she wasn't alone, she was going to die saving someone, she was...

"Watch out!" Nitesh shouted. Pointing ahead.

But he wasn't pointing behind Keira. He was pointing... above.

"The roof!"

Keira looked up.

The roof.

The roof was covered in flames.

And the roof was creaking.

Wobbling.

It was about to fall.

It was about to...

She held her breath and ran as fast as she could as behind her, those screaming figures edged closer.

"Almost there," she muttered. "Almost—almost there—"

And then a huge creaking noise erupted above her.

A bang echoed through the corridor.

And, right behind her, a crash.

She tumbled forward. Fell face flat on the solid hospital floor, Dad right by her side.

She looked over her shoulder.

The hospital roof lay on the floor. Flames crept along it. The sun shone down from the open sky above, as fresh air filled Keira's lungs.

Underneath the fallen roof, two bodies. Both of them twitching. Trying to drag themselves from underneath. Teeth snapping. Snarling. But no chance of getting out from underneath. No chance of escape.

Keira turned around. Dad lay beside her.

She grabbed him. Helped him limp up to his feet.

"It's okay," she said. "I've got you. We've got this."

He looked up into her eyes. Smiled, tears filling his bloodshot eyes.

"I thought I'd lost you," he said. "I thought I'd lost you, my dear."

And Keira looked away. Before the emotion could grow any stronger, she looked away. Tried to hold back the tears. "We're okay," she said. "Everything's going to be okay."

She held Dad's arm, and she looked out at the sunlight outside the hospital.

She looked at Nitesh, standing there, the kids by his side. And this dog, this Golden Retriever, wagging its tail as her and Dad approached.

And then she heard the sirens. She heard the screams. She heard helicopters in the sky. She heard crashing, and smashing, everywhere. Saw smoke plumes rising all over. And behind her, right behind her, the heat from the flames of a collapsing hospital, a constant reminder of what she'd been through, of what she'd almost fallen victim to.

She looked back at the hospital. At the flames. At the smoke. Then at the figures still inside there, in the windows of floors high up; floors way out of reach. And tears fell down her cheeks. The people who hadn't been so lucky. The people she hadn't been able to help.

And then she looked at the kids.

Then at Dad.

Dad looked back at her. Wheezing. Limping. But looking right at her, tears in his eyes.

She looked at him. And she smiled.

Then she turned around to face the chaos of the world ahead.

She might've escaped the hospital.

But Keira had a feeling her journey of survival had only just begun.

END OF BOOK 1

Contagion Rising, the second book in The Infected Chronicles series, is now available.

If you want to be notified when Ryan Casey's next novel is released—and receive an exclusive post apocalyptic novel totally free—sign up for the author newsletter: ryancaseybooks.com/fanclub

Printed in Great Britain
by Amazon